The Adventures of Robin Hood and Marian

Retold by
Adrian Mitchell

Illustrated by
Emma Chichester Clark

ORCHARD BOOKS

James Begotten
Little John

A Monkey
Harrietta

Lady Rosabella
The Sheriff's Wife

Robert Locksley
Robin Hood

William Stutely
Will Scarlett

Contents

Adrian Mountain
Alan A-Dale

The Dogs
Stubbs and Hayrick

The Sheriff
of Nottingham

Friar Michael
Friar Tuck

Sir Ralph
Montfalcon

Lady Matilda Fitzwater
Maid Marian

Baron Fitzwater
Father of Lady Matilda

The Hoghigs
Jenny and Jemmy Scuttle

A Cat
Helena

Now as through this world I ramble,
I see lots of funny men,
Some will rob you with a six gun,
And some with a fountain pen.

But as through this life you travel,
And as through your life you roam,
You won't never see an outlaw
Drive a family from their home.

Woody Guthrie, from the song 'Pretty Boy Floyd'

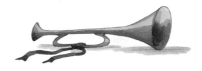

Where the Stories Come From

I read many Robin Hood books before writing *Robin Hood and Marian*. The ones I liked best were *Maid Marian*, which Thomas Love Peacock published in 1822, and *The Merry Adventures of Robin Hood*, which the American Quaker, Howard Pyle wrote and illustrated and published in 1883 and is still obtainable in an edition by Dover Books. These are storybooks, but the most useful historical works, if you are going to find out how true the stories are, will be *Robin Hood: A Complete Study of the English Outlaw* by Stephen Knight (Blackwell, 1994) and Robin Hood by J. C. Holt (Thames & Hudson, 1982). You should also read the ballads about Robin in *The Oxford Book of Ballads* and hear Woody Guthrie's wonderful song about Pretty Boy Floyd, a Wild West Robin Hood. Like every other writer of stories about Robin, I have invented some stories and characters.

Was There Really a Robin Hood?

There were hundreds of Robin Hoods. In the Middle Ages most of England was covered with forest. The laws of the land were harsh and there were many outlaws who lived by robbing travellers. Many of them used the name of Robin Hood so nobody would know their real name. Who was the first Robin Hood? Read my book and find out for yourself.

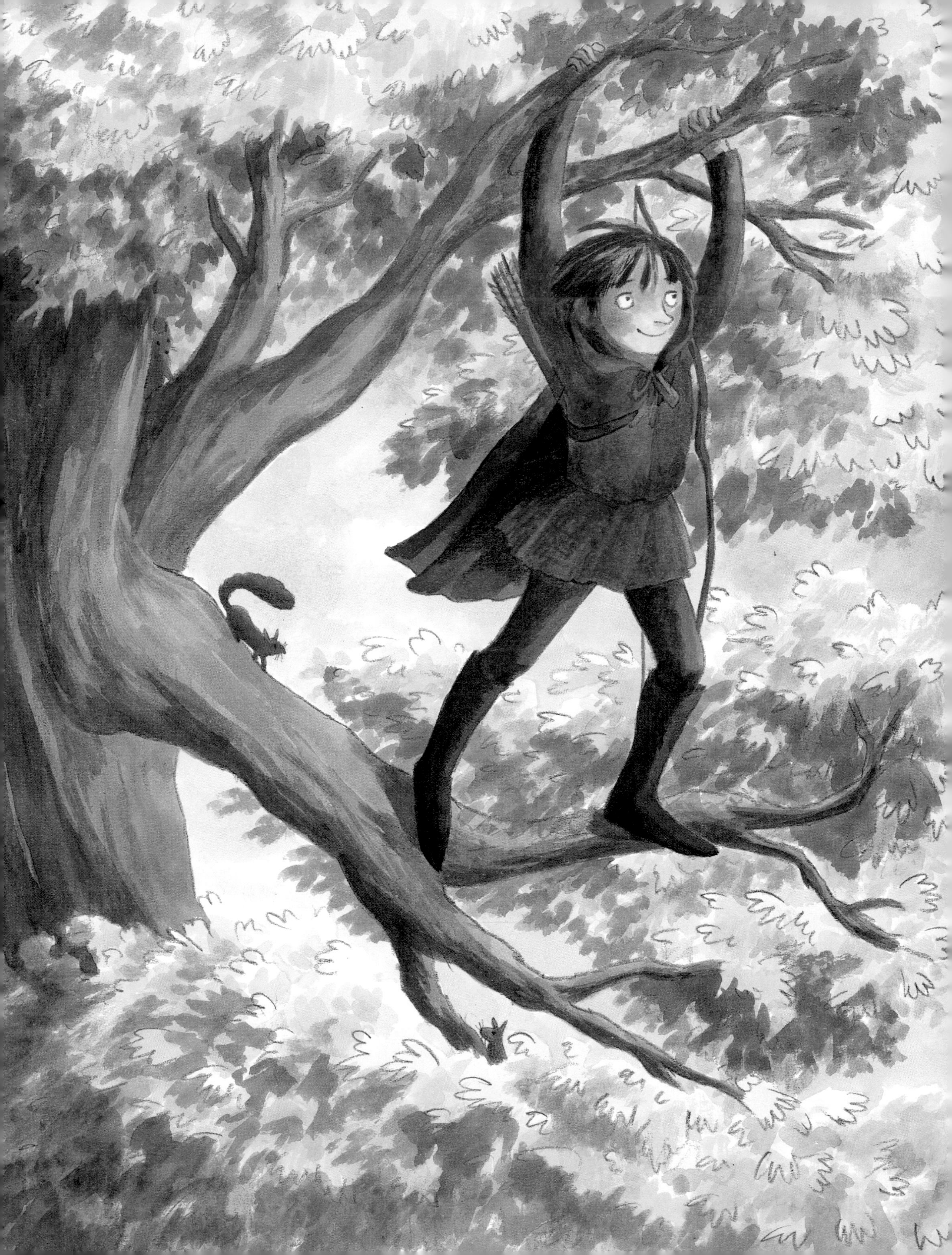

The Runaway

When Robin was nine years old, he ran away from home and went to live in a tree.

It was a big old oak tree, near the edge of Sherwood Forest. Round the back of its trunk it had this hole about the size of a sheep. If you were brave enough, you could climb right into the tree.

Robin jumped in. It was dark. The black earth floor was all crumbly. There was a smell of damp dogs. But it was secret. It was safe.

He put down his pack of food and his bow and arrow. Then he stood inside the hollow tree. When he looked upwards there was a circle of light, like he was in a chimney. He stuck his back against one side of that wooden chimney, his boots on the other side.

Bit by bit, Robin pushed himself up and into and through that circle of light. He sprawled out on to a platform between three enormous boughs. The platform was the size of a rowboat. There were so many green leaves around him, all he could see was green.

Now he was up and into the arms of the tree, Robin began to climb. He was skinny and strong. And he swung to the top of that tree like the king of all the monkeys.

When he reached the top of the oak, it was swaying like the topmast of a sailing ship. He could see the whole world from up there, mostly. The world was green. Nearly all green, except for Robin's own village, which was brown, and the distant stone city of Nottingham, which was grey.

The sun was hot gold and the world looked good. But Robin felt bad. Anyone can let a fire go out. But Robin was the son of a blacksmith. A smith's fire is his living. Without it he can't shoe a horse or put the tip on an arrow. And should that smithy fire fall to ashes, the blacksmith clouts the clodpole who was meant to keep it flaming.

Robin hadn't stopped to be clouted by his dad. He'd grabbed some food and his bow and arrows and headed for the oak. Nobody could find him so high up, perching in his green breeches, jerkin and hood. He felt proud in his anger, like a young hawk.

A voice nearly made him jump off the branch for his first flying lesson. A squeaky voice from down below: "Bob Locksley! I'm coming up."

"There is no Bob Locksley," said Robin. "Here in the forest men call me Robin Hood." Robin knew who it must be, but he asked anyway. "Is that little Lady Matilda Fitzwater, then? What are you doing so far from your daddy's castle? What use can a girl be in the greenwood?" he said harshly.

There was a fizzing sound past his right ear. An arrow pinned his green hood to the tree. Below him, twanging her bowstring, stood little Lady Matilda with her long black hair. She grinned, showing in her top row of teeth, two small vampire-like fangs and two teeth missing in the middle.

"I'm nearly seven, I can go where I like," she said. "And don't call me Lady anything. Here in the forest men call me Maid Marian."

She nodded, stepped into the hollow oak and scrambled her way up. As she pulled herself up on to the platform, Robin extracted the arrow, then slid down to join her.

"What are you doing here?" he asked.

"I've run away," she said happily. "I heard that you ran away, so I ran away to be with you, Robin, and share your adventures in the forest."

"And my bread and cheese too, I suppose," said Robin.

"Thank you, Robin," said Marian, gazing at him with black-treacle eyes. "I did forget to bring any food. But I brought my bow and some arrows and I can shoot good as any boy. You're glad I came here to share your adventures, aren't you, Robin Hood?"

Robin hadn't reckoned on sharing his adventures with anyone. He couldn't take on the responsibility of looking after a six-year-old.

"Look, Lady Matilda – "

"Maid Marian," she said firmly.

Robin patted her dark hair like an uncle and smiled at her gently. Robin had two kinds of smiles. The one most people knew was a slow, warm smile which sent a sweet arrow through your heart. He had another smile, a very dangerous smile, which he saved for his enemies.

"Look, Maid Marian, I've got to explain something," he said. "If I run away, nobody's worried – I'm just a blacksmith's lad. But if you run away, well, you're the young lady of the castle, you're a little dark diamond. They'll have the Sheriff of Nottingham and his bullies searching every bush and tree in Sherwood till they find you. They'll think I've stolen you away, and they'll hang me a dozen times before they're through."

"They'd really hang you? No." Marian felt very cold. She mustn't put Robin in danger. "I'll say you never stole me."

"They won't believe you," said Robin. "They never believe what children say, ever."

She didn't want him to tell her to go. So she said: "I'll go

home." She didn't cry. She scampered down inside the tree and out of the hole, smart as a squirrel. She waved and sort of grinned up at him.

"Don't run away for long," she called. Then off she ran through the trees and out of sight.

Robin spent six days and six nights in and around the tree. He lived on his bread and cheese washed down with brook water drunk from the palms of his hands.

Nobody saw him. But on the sixth evening he saw somebody. It was his own father, bow and arrow at the ready, standing still as a scarecrow, watching. Robin saw him draw the bow and fire an arrow three hundred paces straight into the heart of a stag. One of the King's own stags. And then he watched as his big father hoisted it up on to his shoulders and carried it away towards home.

The seventh morning a storm came up. Robin began to worry about his mother worrying and about his father being angry and even about little Marian. A week in the woods seemed enough. Especially if there was deer for dinner. He walked jauntily back to Arlington, his village.

Everybody was standing outside their cottages. They stared like ghosts. They said nothing at all to Robin.

Outside his cottage sat his mother, crying to herself with Matilda/Marian holding her hand. Robin squatted beside his mother and put his arm around her and stared into her face, but her mouth was wide open and her eyes were shut tight and squeezing out tears. She couldn't say one word.

But Marian could: "The men came riding with masks on their faces. And they had big swords. And they found your dad roasting a deer. And they said he must be punished for stealing from the King. And they took him inside where he works. And I don't know what they did, but he shouts out. And when they go he is all covered with soot and blood and he can't see any more. And your mother puts her arms round him, and he falls down right here."

"Where is he?" asked Robin.

He went into the smithy. There was his father laid on a table, candles at his head and feet. His big face wasn't red any more. His great hands were clasped on his chest. Robin knelt beside him.

Outside the smithy Marian was still trying to comfort Robin's mother.

"That big man who brought those men in masks, I hated him. He sounded so cruel. When he was climbing back on his horse I bit him on his hand really badly and there was blood. His left hand, not his sword hand. He did have a gold snaky ring on that hand, too. I bit him hard."

Robin was on his knees beside his father's corpse. He thought about how that big man used to sing as he worked in a deep-down voice that seemed to comfort nervous horses. He thought about his mother telling magical stories in the evening and his father listening with smiling eyes. He remembered a hundred and one good times and only two or three bad times. Robin's heart felt as if it was going to explode.

Outlawed

Ten years later, times were still troubled in Sherwood. King Richard, who had promised to protect the people, was never in England. He was always over the seas, fighting the heathen in his Crusades. England was in chaos.

Poor people had the worst of it. By night, gangs of armed men raided their villages with flaming torches and wicked swords. By day, the tax collectors called, demanding money to pay for the great Crusades. But most of the taxes went to the Sheriff of Nottingham, the most powerful man in Sherwood, who delighted in persecuting the poor with cruel laws.

Robin Hood, now nineteen years old, was always in trouble. He was a good blacksmith. Marian and the villagers and wandering beggars and the horses he shoed all adored him. But wealthy priests and nobles were used to humble blacksmiths who worked for nothing. Robin made them pay, cash down. When the Sheriff and his taxmen came, Robin was always over the hills and far away. And he was suspected of hunting and eating the royal deer.

One day the Sheriff of Nottingham announced a great

shooting match. The prize would be a priceless
silver brooch from Araby. As soon as he heard, Robin
picked up his good yew bow and a quiver full of twenty-four
arrows and began the long walk from Arlington through
Sherwood Forest to Nottingham.

It was Maytime, with daisies and primroses everywhere
among the grass, with apple blossom above your head and the
lark and cuckoo singing fit to bust. As Robin walked through
the green shadows of a little winding path, he thought about
Marian and he whistled an old song, only slightly out of tune.

He came to a clearing and stopped. There sat a group of
fifteen men in yellow jerkins, feasting and drinking and
laughing. They sat around a huge pie, helping themselves.

Their leader was a small, stout man with sandy-coloured
hair, a reddish beard and a hat of floppy, dark blue velvet.

He called out to Robin, although his mouth was full: "Hey,
boy, where are you going with that toy bow and arrow?"

The men laughed. Robin didn't.

"I am going to the shooting match at Nottingham to win
the silver brooch from Araby," he said coldly. The man in
the blue hat laughed and so did all his followers.

"Listen to the lad," said the hat man. "Your mother's milk
isn't dry on your lips and you talk about drawing the string of
a longbow against the strongest men in Nottingham!"

"I will bet you five pounds," said Robin, "that I can hit any
target you name, however small, at five hundred paces."

Blue Hat smiled. "Any target at all?" he asked.

"Any target," said Robin. "A crabapple, a daffodil stem –
even your abominable hat, sir."

"Agreed, agreed!" said the hat man, shoving out a large
white clammy fist and shaking Robin's hand. "Five pounds."

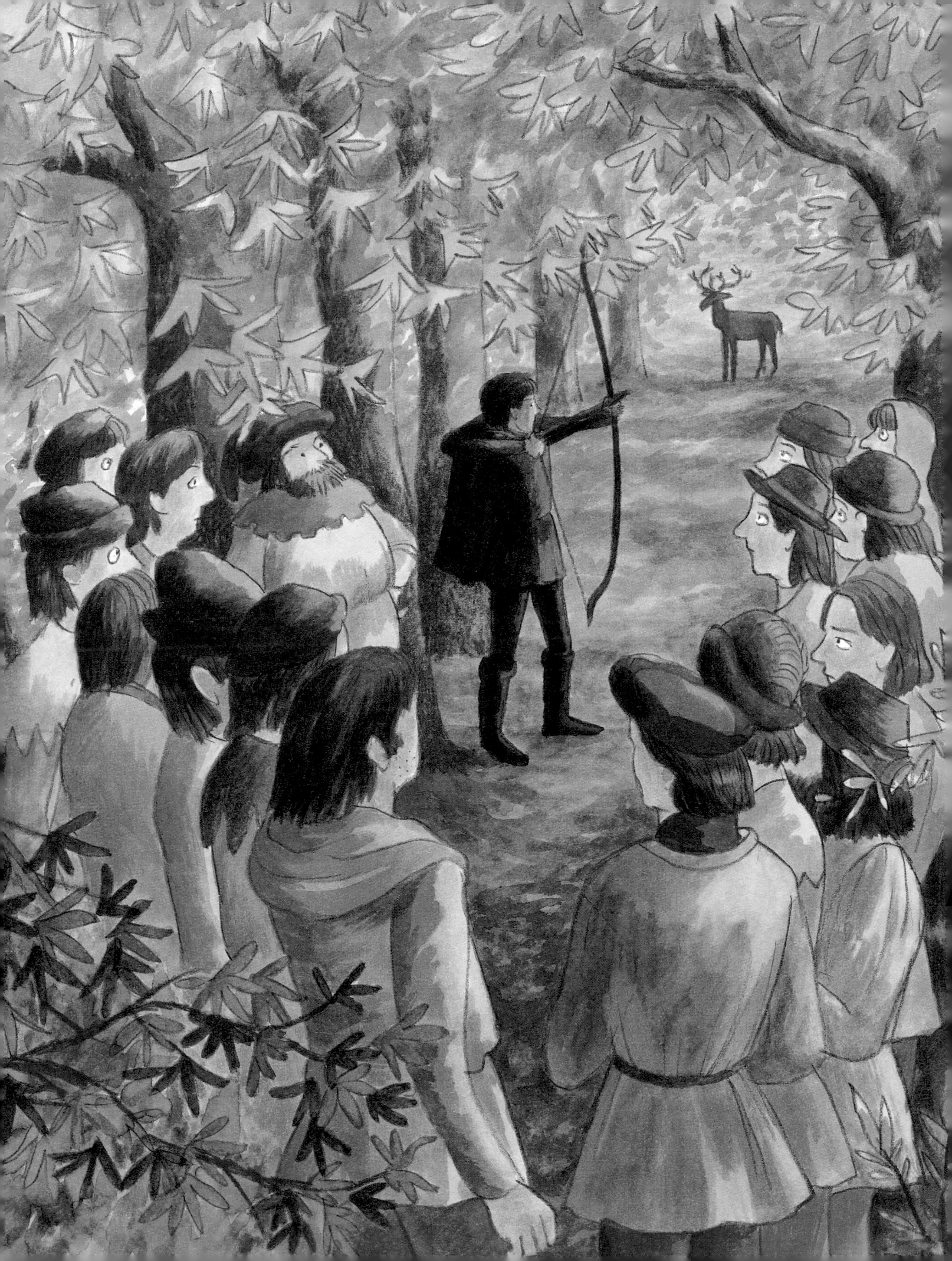

"What's the target?" asked Robin.

The man pointed to the far end of the clearing. A large deer was grazing, its antlers brushing the grass. "The stag," he said. His men began to chant: "The stag! The stag! The stag! The stag!"

Robin remembered how his father had been viciously murdered for the killing of a stag. But Robin would prove he was as brave as his father.

He stopped himself from listening to the chanting of the men. He strung his great bow. He placed the notch of an arrow on the string. He raised the bow and drew the grey goose feather to his ear.

The bowstring rang. The arrow flew across the clearing. The stag leapt and fell, with Robin's arrow in his heart. Robin walked to it, made sure it was dead, then turned back and called: "Was that good, Mister Hat? I'll thank you for my five pounds."

But the stout man sat down comfortably on a tree stump and stroked his ginger beard.

"I do hope you understand what you have done, boy," he said. "You appear to have killed one of the King's deer. I'm sure you know the penalties for such an offence, Bob Locksley, for your father paid dearly for the same crime."

"You know me? Is this a trap?"

"That's right. I am the Sheriff of Nottingham and you are Bob Locksley alias Robin Hood and you are under arrest. Take him!"

But Robin had strung an arrow and let it fly. It caught the dark blue velvet hat and carried it fifty paces, nailing it to a tree. Before a man moved, Robin had strung a second arrow.

"My second arrow is for the Sheriff's belly," said Robin. He aimed it very carefully and smiled his dangerous smile. "Now all of you men stay exactly where you are and don't move. Sheriff, stand up and walk over to me."

One arrow commanded every man in the clearing. The Sheriff walked towards it as if hypnotised. Robin kept his aim on that shaking belly.

"Five pounds," said Robin.

The Sheriff drew five gold sovereigns from his purse and placed it on the ground.

"And I'll take the silver brooch," said Robin.

A grim-faced Sheriff handed it over. Robin gave that red beard a contemptuous tug.

"Now get down on your hands and knees and crawl back to your men," said Robin.

"Yes," said the Sheriff as he obeyed. "You will pay most terribly for this."

"Well worth it," said Robin.

As the Sheriff reached his men, Robin turned and ran for his life. Wild arrows fell around him, but he laughed as he ran home.

"But that's pure silver, that must be for your Lady Matilda," said the Widow Locksley, flustered, as her son pinned the brooch to her dress.

"You can leave it to her in your will," said Robin and ducked as his mother tried to cuff him round the side of the head.

As soon as the Sheriff arrived home in Nottingham he proclaimed Robert Locksley to be an outlaw. Any man who found him would be rewarded for his killing or capture. For the second time in his life Robin went to live in the forest.

But this time he was not alone. In Sherwood Forest he made many friends. Some had been outlawed for shooting deer in winter when no other food could be found. Some had been turned off their farms so that the Sheriff of Nottingham could take their lands. Some had their money and animals taken by a roaming band of knights or by the abbot of the local monastery.

Together they vowed to take revenge on those who had wronged them, and to take back the money that had been stolen from them. They also swore that they would help all those in need or trouble and would never do harm to any woman or child or poor man.

21

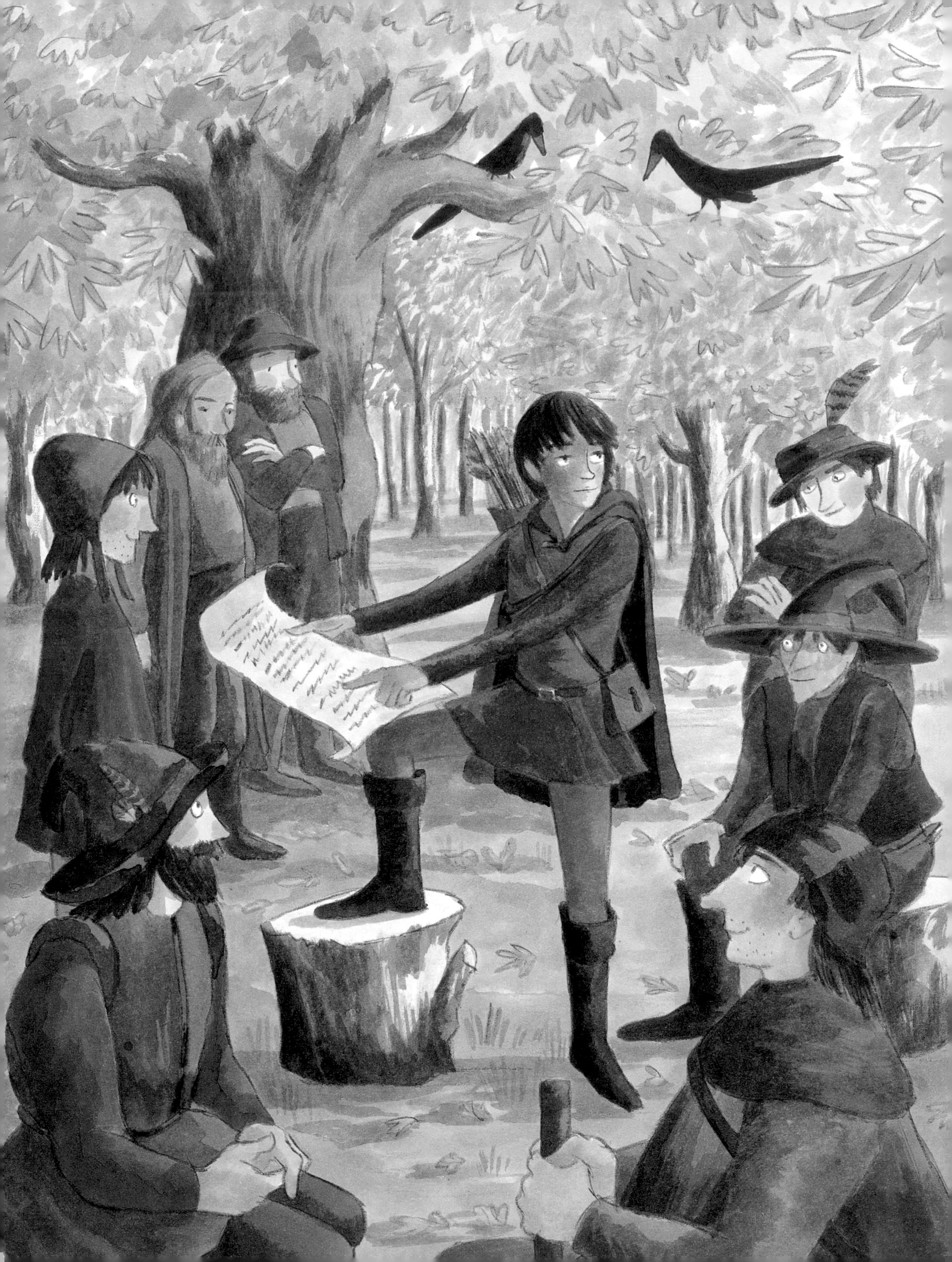

In a forest glade, Robin declared these new laws of the forest to his fellow outlaws.

1. The forest is a free forest. All the old forest laws are abolished. We have the right to keep what we have and to catch what we can.

2. The rich have too much and the poor have too little, mainly because the rich have all kinds of cunning and brutal ways of robbing the poor. As outlaws we pledge ourselves to take from the rich and give to the poor.

3. We will protect and aid all women and children and orphans and all those who are weak or sick or distressed.

4. All carriers of messages and market traders and peasants, mechanics, farmers, millers and blacksmiths shall pass through our forest in freedom.

5. All other travellers through the forest shall be invited politely to dine with Robin, whether they are willing or no. The poor shall feast for nothing. But the rich man, whether he is a lord or a tax-collector or priest or monk or sheriff shall pay dearly for his dinner.

All the outlaws swore to maintain these laws. It was not long before the people grew to love Robin Hood and his men and to sing songs and tell stories about their brave adventures in Sherwood Forest.

A Wild Wedding

Every man, woman, child, baby and dog in the village of Arlington washed its face and paws and paraded noisily up the hill to the Baron's castle. They all knew the wild young Lady Matilda and not one of them would miss the fun and feasting of her wedding. The genial, plump figure of Friar Michael greeted each one of them with a kiss or a pat or a shake of the hand as they poured into the castle chapel.

Once inside, their babbling fell to a whispering. The great organ with its golden pipes hummed, moaned and howled. Thin columns of scented smoke rose towards the vaulted ceiling. The scruffiest boy in the village, robed in white, stepped forward and sang an anthem like the flying of angels.

Baron Fitzwater was a kindly but short-tempered man, who loved his castle and his food. Friar Michael beamed as he welcomed the nervous Baron and his daughter Lady Matilda to the foot of the altar. The bride wore clouds of white lace. Were it not for her veil you could have seen that now, at the age of seventeen, she had perfect teeth. Her small bridesmaids arranged her train, giggled together and were led to one side by a scolding aunt.

But where was the groom? The Baron caught his fat Friar by the sleeve.

"What's happened to that rapscallion? I knew I shouldn't let him marry my daughter."

"You had no choice," said the Friar. "Lady Matilda, as you well know, obeys nothing but her own will. Besides, the boy has a noble heart."

"Noble!" said the Baron. "He's the village blacksmith. Nothing noble about a blacksmith. And late for his wedding. Is that the act of a gentleman?"

The Friar had no time to answer. Everyone turned at the sound of running feet and there was Robin, sword at his side, dusty, sweaty and smiling as he ran up the aisle and took the hand of his bride, who squeezed it and stuck out her tongue at him, under cover of her veil.

Friar Michael began to chant the ceremony, singing through his nose. And a very musical nose it was. He was enjoying his own singing when it was rudely interrupted by a clanking sound as a party of armed men, led by the huge figure of Sir Ralph Montfalcon, strode up the aisle.

Everybody in Arlington knew Sir Ralph. He was the fiercest tax gatherer in England and he kept most of what he gathered for himself.

Sir Ralph wore armour bright enough to blind you. He was

tall and wide and wore his visor up, so everyone could see his staring blue eyes and yellow moustache. He drew his sword and stepped in between Robin and Marian.

Sir Ralph spoke: "In the name of Prince John, I forbid this ceremony. I hereby arrest Robert Locksley as an outlaw and a traitor."

Robin's sword flashed and struck Sir Ralph's weapon to the stone floor. He put his left arm around Marian and held his sword in his right, ready to strike.

"My children," said the Friar, "if you must cut each other's throats, I beg you, by the bright eyes of Saint Dorothea, to do it outside this chapel."

Robin looked at his bride, keeping his guard up all the time. "Sweet Lady Matilda, sweet Maid Marian, do you give me all your love for ever?"

She raised her veil and smiled. "Sweet Robert Locksley, sweet Robin Hood, I give you all my love for as long as there are trees in Sherwood."

Robin kissed her lips and she kissed him back. Then he stepped away from her, raised his sword, and charged towards the mass of twenty soldiers which packed the aisle.

"Cut down the outlaw!" shouted Sir Ralph. He tried to pick up his sword. But the fat Friar was standing on its blade, staring at a stained-glass window and smiling to himself.

It could have been a very brief and bloody battle. But at the last moment Robin swerved into a crowded pew, pushing his way past the startled people. Halfway along, he stepped on to a wooden bench and then moved in a series of great strides from the back of one pew to the next as if they were stepping-stones. Twenty pews he stepped across, though now and then he had to use somebody's shoulder.

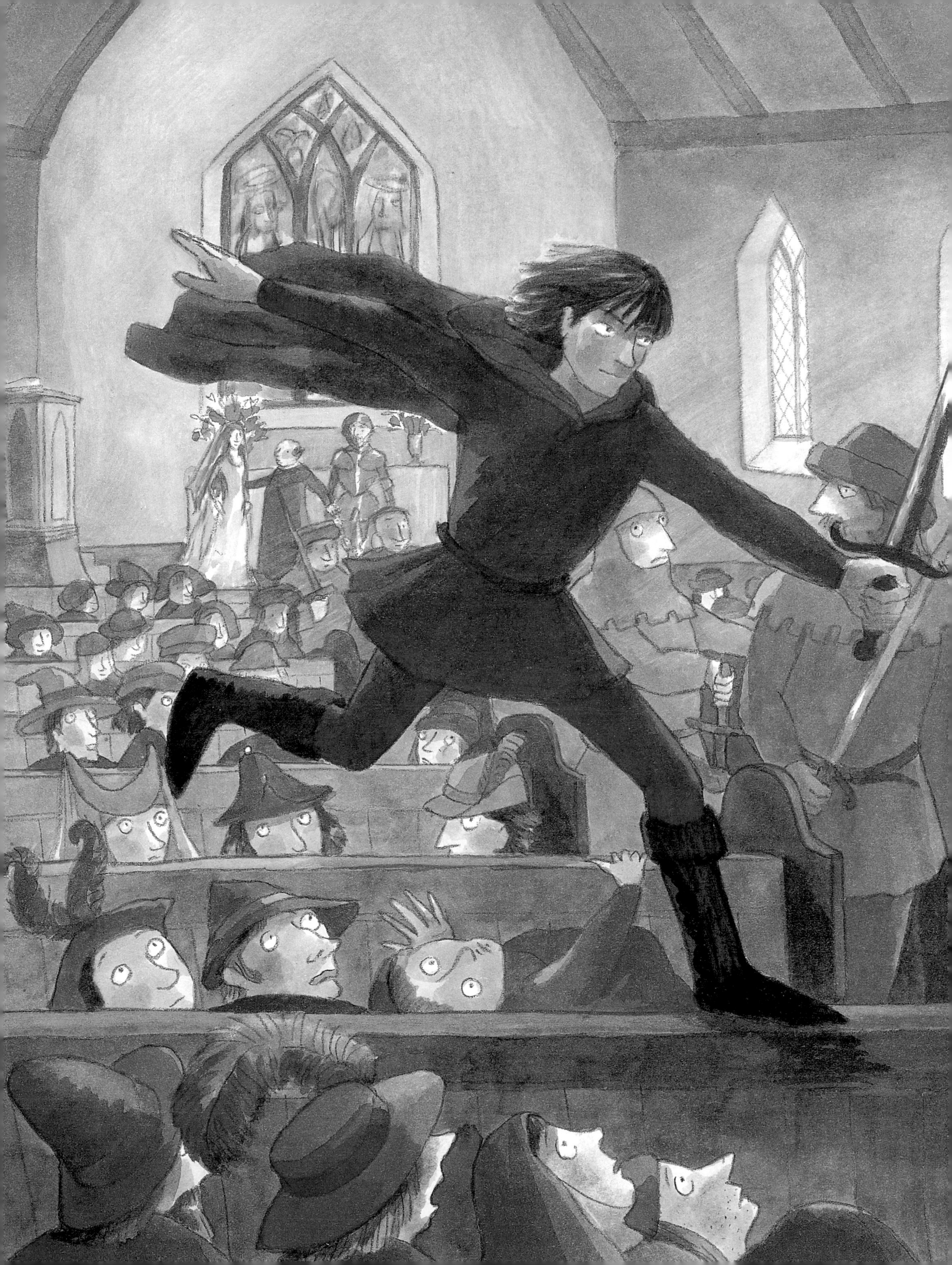

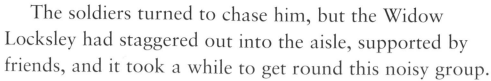

The soldiers turned to chase him, but the Widow Locksley had staggered out into the aisle, supported by friends, and it took a while to get round this noisy group.

By this time Robin was out of the chapel door, on to a horse and galloping towards the greenwood. A volley of arrows followed him, but they were too late. He was so fast that the congregation didn't start screaming and fainting until he was gone.

The bride stood at the door of the chapel waving until her groom was out of sight. Then she went back to her room in the castle and played a game of chess against herself while she made exciting plans for the future.

A Big Little Man

It was early morning in Sherwood. Springtime sunshine broke through the leaves. A cool breeze, like a dog, licked Robin's cheek. All his men were asleep except the cheerful, cunning Will Scarlett, who stood guard.

Robin whispered to Will: "We haven't had any real fun for two weeks. I'm going off by myself to find adventure."

"You may find yourself arrested and dropped in the Sheriff's Bottle Dungeon," said Will. "There's a bag of gold sovereigns for the man who catches you."

Robin grinned. "They'll be lucky. Anyway, if I'm in trouble I'll blow three blasts on my bugle." He strode off through the maze of trees. Two hours later he was walking along a sandy path at the edge of Sherwood.

He met a miller's daughter and swapped a couple of jokes. He saw a grand lady on an ambling white mare and took off his green cap. He waved to a skinny monk on a fat donkey. He stood well back among the leaves, watching as a gallant knight rode by, his armour flashing brightly in the sun. He met some fishermen, old friends of his, who gave him

29

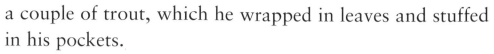

a couple of trout, which he wrapped in leaves and stuffed in his pockets.

All these people he saw and a hundred animals and birds as well, but he couldn't find any adventure at all. Finally he took a path that dipped towards a broad and pebbly stream crossed by a narrow bridge made out of the fallen trunk of a tree. As he walked up to this bridge he saw a tall, wide-shouldered stranger coming from the other side.

Robin walked more quickly. So did the stranger. Each of them wanted to be first across. They stopped. Each had one foot placed on the bridge.

"Stand back and let a better man cross," shouted Robin.

"No," called out the stranger in a deep voice. "Stand back yourself, for I'm the better man by far."

"We'll see about that," said Robin. "Stand back or I'll tickle your ribs with an arrow."

The big man raised a six-foot wooden staff and twirled it round his head with fingers big as sausages.

"You stand back, or I'll use my quarterstaff to tan your skin as many colours as a patchwork quilt," he said.

"That's donkey talk," said Robin, "for I could send this arrow clean through your heart before you could scratch your dripping nose."

"That's coward talk," said the big man, "to use a longbow against a man with only a staff."

"Nobody ever used the word coward to me before," said Robin angrily. "If you dare wait for me, I'll go and cut myself a club to test your courage and your skull."

"I am very happy to wait," said the stranger. He watched lazily as Robin cut himself a good oak staff, six feet long, and trimmed the twigs from it.

30

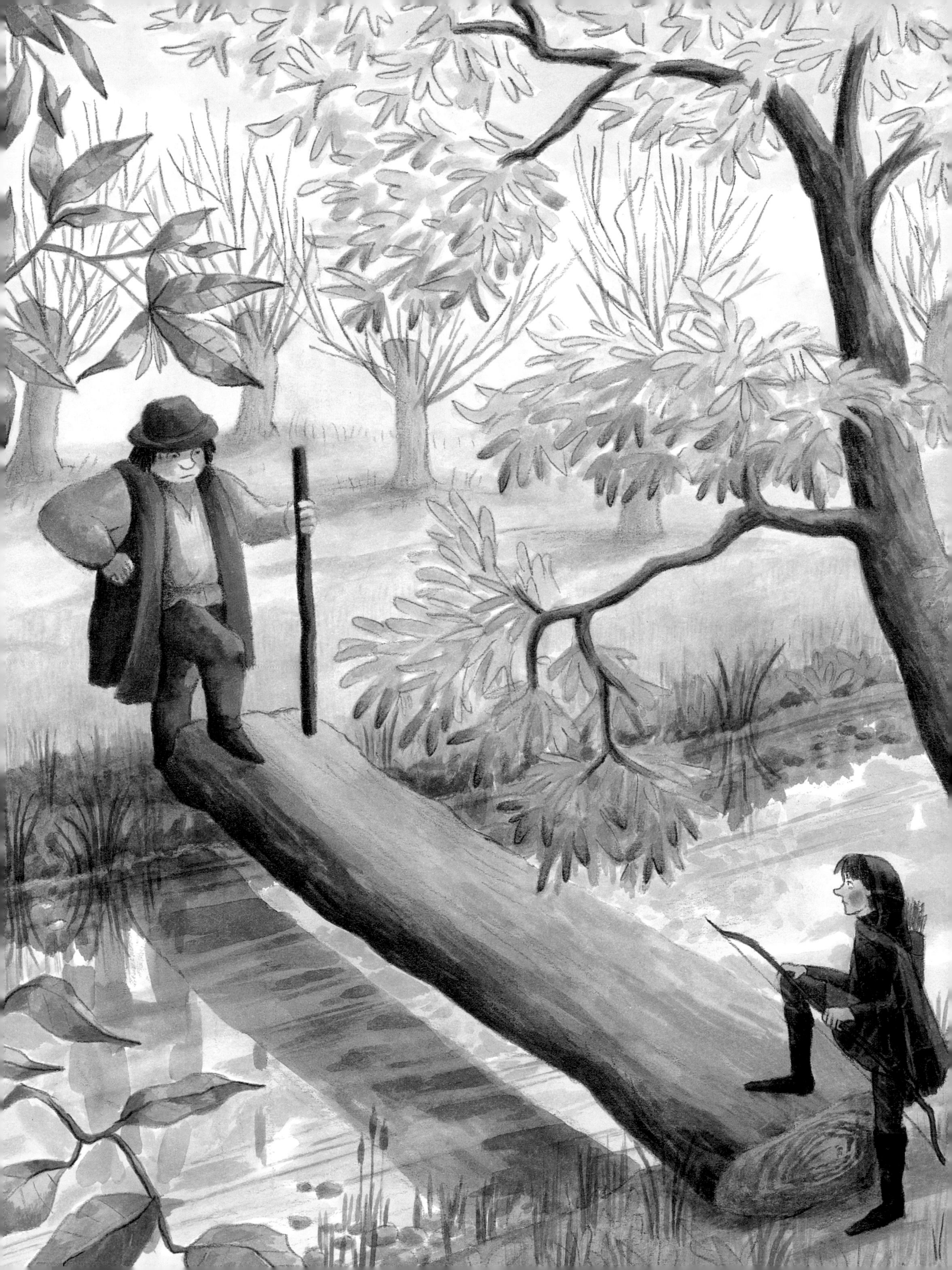

As he worked, Robin glanced at the other man out of the corner of his eye. Robin was tall, but this man was taller by a head and a neck. He must be seven feet high. His chest and his back were huge. But Robin could move quicker than a lizard and strike more swiftly than an adder.

Robin was ready. "Come on," he said. "We'll fight till one or the other of us falls in this stream."

"Delighted," said the big man, twirling his staff between his finger and thumb so rapidly that it whistled through the air. The two men stared, then began to walk towards each other over the rough bridge.

Soon they were head-to-head. Robin pretended to strike to the left, then whirled his staff to the right, straight at the big man's forehead. But his opponent blocked the blow with his staff and hit back. Robin's staff neatly turned this to one side.

And so, as the sun rose towards a baking noonday, the two men stood toe-to-toe, neither of them moving an inch backwards. They stood there battling for a whole hour. Many blows were given and received by each of them. Both were covered with bumps and bruises and their bones were aching. But neither fighter even thought of crying out "Enough!"

Now and then they would stop to rest for a few seconds. Each man knew he had never faced such an excellent player of the painful game of quarterstaff.

At last Robin gave the stranger a blow on the ribs that made him lurch off balance, and for a second it seemed sure he must fall off the bridge. But he swung back and, standing like a tower, gave Robin a crack on the head. Blood began to roll down Robin's forehead. Robin was angry. He hit back with huge force, but the big man swayed to one side and Robin hurtled past him to tumble, head over heels, into the rushing water.

"Come back," said the big man. "I haven't finished with you yet."

"Give me your hand," said Robin when he reached the bank. "I admit that you're a brave fellow and wickedly cunning with that staff of yours. My poor head's humming like a beehive."

The big man pulled him out. Once he was safe on the grass, Robin put his bugle to his lips and blew three times.

"You put up a brave fight," said the big man, "but what's the music for?"

He soon found out. A few minutes later there was a rustling in the forest and suddenly he was surrounded by a dozen armed men in Lincoln green led by Will Scarlett.

"What's this, Robin?" said Will. "You're soaked from head to foot."

"Right," said Robin. "That monster bashed me with his staff and then tumbled me into the water."

"Then we'll see how he likes being thumped and ducked, won't we, boys?" said Will.

"Listen," said Robin, "he is a right good man and a true one. None of you must hurt him. Big man, will you stay with me in Sherwood Forest and be one of my gang? You will have three suits of Lincoln green every year and share with us in whatever we find or take. You shall eat venison, the sweet meat of the King's deer, and drink good ale. And you shall be my right-hand man, for I never saw a better man with a staff in all my life. Come on, will you be one of my men?"

"You fought a brave fight," said the big man, "I grant you that. I'll join your good company."

Everybody cheered.

"I've gained a good man today," said Robin. "What do they call you?"

"I'm James Begotten," said the man.

"Oh no," said Will Scarlett, "you must take a forest name. What shall we call you? I know, because you're such a tiny midge of a fellow, we'll call you Little John."

"You make fun of me and your skeleton will soon be in a hundred pieces," said John angrily.

"Bottle up your anger," said Robin, "the name suits you. From now on we shall all call you Little John."

They took him back to the great oak tree which Robin had known since he was a boy. Nearby, up in the treetops and down in the undergrowth, Robin's men had made huts of bark and tents of deerskin. A fire was built and a feast prepared and the big man sat at the right hand of Robin Hood. By the time the feast had ended they were all the best of friends and the new outlaw was very happy to be known by his new name – Little John.

Marian Decides

Baron Fitzwater was dining with Friar Michael when Sir Ralph Montfalcon burst into the hall unannounced.

"Apologies for disturbing your feast," said Sir Ralph, "but I wanted to explain my interruption of your daughter's wedding."

The Baron didn't mix food and explanations. He liked to chew his roast beef and swig his wine and maybe talk afterwards if he hadn't fallen asleep. And he didn't fancy being stared at by this big, intruding knight with his bulging blue eyes, long yellow locks of hair on his balding head and a yellow moustache to match. But he was a polite Baron, so he ordered a trencher of beef and a goblet of Canary wine for his uninvited guest.

"Lord Fitzwater," said Sir Ralph, "in obedience to the High Sheriff of Nottingham, I stopped your daughter's marriage. Otherwise she would now be the wife of a famous outlaw."

"Most kind of you," said the Baron, sarcastically, "to take such an interest in my daughter's future. I'm obviously incapable of looking after her myself."

"I'm sorry," said Sir Ralph. "If I had realised that you wanted her to marry that outlaw, I would have waited for him outside the chapel."

"I don't want her to marry an outlaw. I don't want him to be an outlaw. But if I wanted her to marry the devil himself, I'd like to see the man who dared interfere."

Sir Ralph turned to the Friar. "Good Friar," he said, "I understand that you are Lady Matilda's tutor."

"I try to teach her, yes," said the Friar. A black cat with a mask of white fur around her eyes jumped from nowhere on to his broad right shoulder and perched there, nodding wisely.

"Then will you persuade her to give up this outlaw?"

"By the dancing legs of Saint Wilhelmina, shall I persuade the river Trent to run uphill, or make an oak tree grow with its branches in the earth and its roots in the air?" replied the Friar, pouring himself another goblet of wine. "Let the young man pay for the deer he killed and be merciful to him, sir."

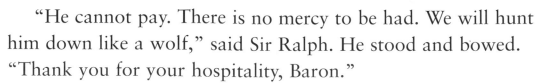

"He cannot pay. There is no mercy to be had. We will hunt him down like a wolf," said Sir Ralph. He stood and bowed. "Thank you for your hospitality, Baron."

Two small, extremely hairy dogs under the table growled as Sir Ralph left the hall. Friar Michael rebuked them. "Hayrick! Stubbs! Save your jaws to chew your paws." The growling stopped. The black cat curled herself round Friar Michael's neck like a dark velvet scarf. "Good Helena," purred the Friar.

"Don't like him," said the Baron, whose stomach was rumbling dangerously. "Don't like Sir Ralph. Don't like Bob Locksley either. Half marrying Matilda. Doesn't look good. Looks bad. Friar Michael, tell her she must never see that young man again."

"Tell her yourself," said a strong young voice, and there was Lady Matilda standing in the doorway. She was wearing everyday green, a quiver at her side and a bow in her hand. Her hair was black as a raven's wing. Hayrick and Stubbs ran to her, wagging their bottoms off.

"What are you doing with that bow and arrow?" asked her father.

"I'm going hunting," she said. "Get down, you silly dogs."

"Hunting indeed!" shouted the Baron. "Hunting that Locksley boy, no doubt, so you can be hanged in the same noose. You shall not leave the castle."

"Father, you can't coop me up here. I'll pine away and die like a lonely swan on a pool."

"You've been reading too much poetry," said the Baron. "Lonely swans don't die on pools. They flap off to the nearest river and find a mate. But you're not going to do that."

"Very well," said Matilda/Marian, "then send me guarded by my good tutor, Friar Michael."

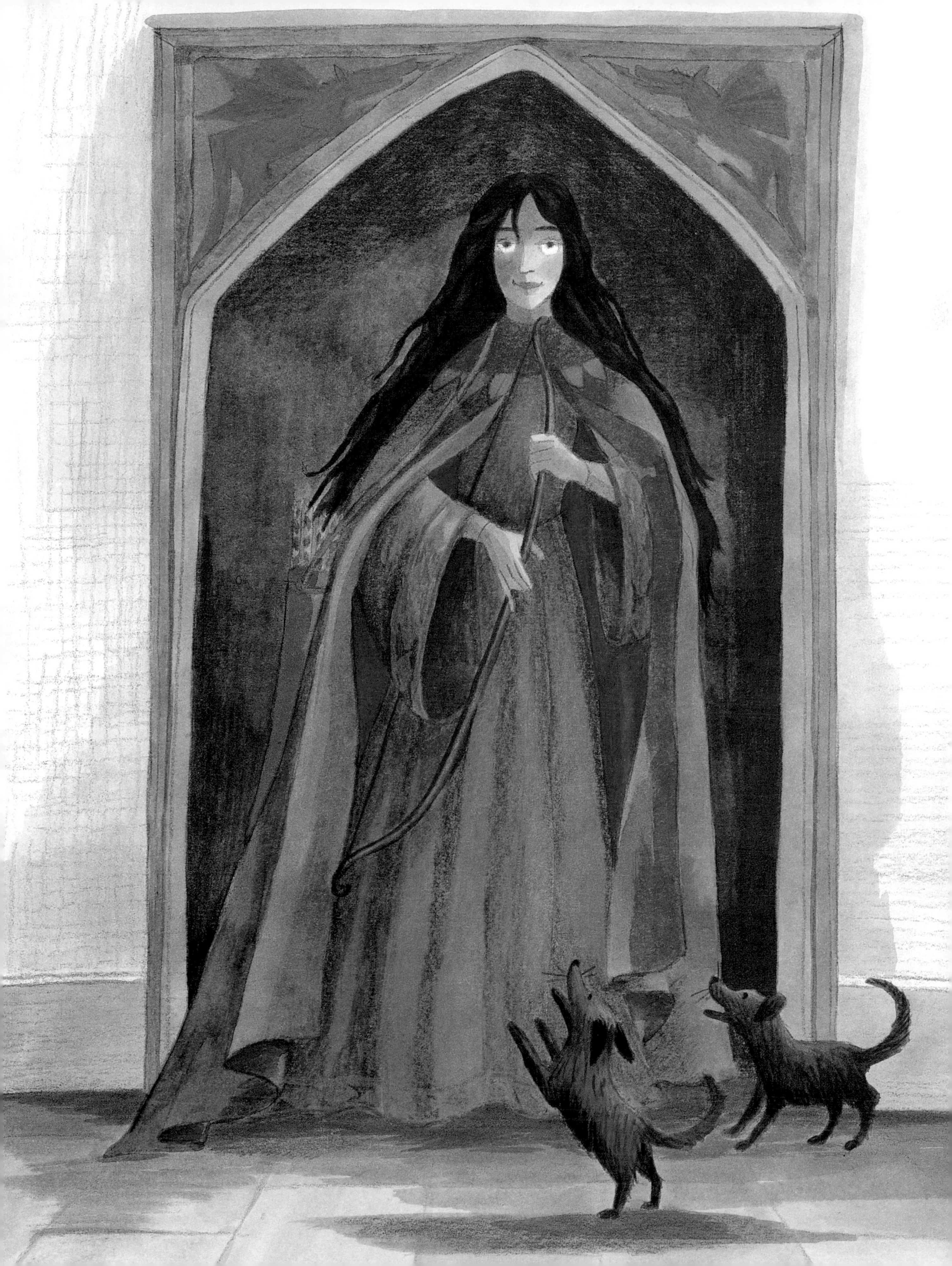

"But the Friar loves you better than he loves me," said the Baron. "He will do whatever you say. You must not see Locksley. He is a poacher and an outlaw."

"He killed a deer," said Matilda. "You're always saying that the laws of the forest are stupid and cruel."

"The boy's not a gentleman. He hasn't got a house. He hasn't any land."

"He has the whole of Sherwood Forest," she said. "Which reminds me, I am off to the woods."

"Oh, no," said the Baron.

"I'm going," said Matilda.

"I will have the drawbridge pulled up."

"Then I'll swim the moat."

"I will lock the gates."

"Then I'll jump from the battlements."

"I'll lock you in an upper room."

"Then I'll tear the tapestry into shreds and knot it into a rope and climb down."

"She will, you know," said Friar Michael. It was the wrong thing to say at the wrong time. The Baron exploded.

"You no-good Friar, you teach my daughter to be a flibbertigibbet and your hairy little dogs raid my larder and you drink more of my wine than all the rest of my servants put together – "

"Pardon me," said the Friar, "but I am not your servant. I am tutor to your daughter and I am proud of her learning and her character."

Helena purred her agreement.

"Did I say I was ashamed of her?" shouted the Baron.

Matilda sat beside him and pulled his beard gently. This usually worked. A smile began at each corner of his mouth. She spoke softly.

"Let's have a peace treaty, Father. During the day I shall be free to visit the forest. But every evening, at dusk, I shall return to you in the castle. I give you the promise of my heart."

She had never broken a promise in her life. The Baron sighed and shook his head a dozen times. So Marian knew that he meant yes.

The Golden Arrow

The Sheriff of Nottingham's castle was a horrible place. It was gloomy and damp and draughty and cold. The only decorations were spiders' webs in summer and icicles in winter.

The most horrible place in the castle was the Bottle Dungeon, of which we shall hear much later. But the second most horrible place was the castle kitchen.

It was a great dark cave of a room, full of steam and flames and screaming and shouting and swearing and sobbing. It was ruled over by a giant cook with an enormous red nose and hairy fists as big as hams.

He was the biggest bully, but all the kitchen staff were bullies in that stenchpit hell of a kitchen. All except for the two smallest – the nine-year-old twins Jenny and Jemmy Scuttle – for there was nobody small enough for them to bully, except the kitchen cat Sparks, and they were fond of her.

Jenny and Jemmy were the children of an African soldier killed in the Crusades. They took more punches and kicks and pinches than anyone else in the castle, and worked ten times as hard.

But one day Jenny and Jemmy found themselves alone in the kitchen. They looked at each other and nodded. Ever since they were captured in Palestine, they had planned for this moment.

Quickly they filled their pockets with bread and cheese, ran down to the cellar, forced an ancient door which led to a tunnel, crawled down the tunnel which ran under the moat and jumped out into freedom. Then they were off into the depths of the wildwood.

That day the Sheriff wanted to discuss the problem of Robin Hood and his gang. More and more bishops and tax collectors were being robbed and insulted by the outlaws.

The Sheriff decided to seek out Sir Ralph Montfalcon. He found him in a smelly little tavern called *The Hanged Man*. Big Sir Ralph was at the dice with a few vicious-looking sailors. He was gambling and, as usual, losing. The Sheriff drew him aside, poured two glasses of wine and explained his difficulty.

Scratching his yellow moustache with sharp and grimy fingernails, Sir Ralph thought for a nasty moment.

"Ha!" he said suddenly, making the Sheriff jump. "I have it. Before a fortnight is up, that Hood fellow-me-lad shall be clapped up in your famous Bottle Dungeon."

"But how?" asked the Sheriff.

"What is the weakness of Robin Hood? Pride. He is proud of being the finest archer who ever drew longbow. So play upon his weakness. Declare a great archery competition and offer some grand prize – perhaps a golden arrow. Hold the contest in the market square of Nottingham. And when Robin, out of his foolhardiness, appears to shoot – pounce!"

"But where do I get a golden arrow?"

"I'll have one made for you. Give me the money – two, no, three gold pounds." As the Sheriff handed over the money, Sir Ralph sucked his moustache happily. He always liked to make a little profit.

So messengers were sent north, south, east and west to proclaim the great shooting match. The Scuttle twins, hiding in a tree at a crossroads, heard a cobbler and a baker talking about the contest. It sounded very exciting.

Jenny and Jemmy travelled on through the woods. At last they were exhausted and crept into a great hollow tree to sleep.

It was there that Little John found them, pulled them out and held them up in the air by their collars.

"Look what I found," he shouted to the other outlaws as they sat around the fire. "Two young spies from the Sheriff of Nottingham's castle. They were hidden away in Robin's oak, snoring like a couple of hedgehogs."

"We're nobody's spies," said Jenny.

"We ran away from the castle," said Jemmy.

"We hate the Sheriff," said Jenny.

"And we're not hoghigs," said Jemmy indignantly.

"We're Jenny and Jemmy Scuttle," said Jenny.

Marian marched over to Little John.

"Put those children down at once. I'll have no bullying in Sherwood."

Little John paused. Marian threatened him with a big soup ladle and he lowered the twins to the ground.

Over some good soup Little John scoffed at the small, scruffy twins. "What use are children to a bunch of bandits?" he asked.

But his laughter stopped as soon as it began. Without his noticing, Jenny and Jemmy had lifted Little John's sword and dagger from the scabbards on his belt and they pricked his legs with them till he danced. Even he had to admit that such light-fingered little thieves might be useful to the gang.

"If you're to join us," said Robin, "you must have new names."

Marian looked at the twins with their spiky, sticky-up hair. "We will name you the Hoghigs," she said and everyone agreed.

It was then the young Hoghigs told the gang all about the great archery contest in Nottingham.

"Listen," said Robin, "the Sheriff's shooting match is good news. I would like one of us to win that golden arrow."

Will Scarlett was doubtful. "This sounds like a trap, Robin, a trap to catch you."

"It probably is a trap, but it doesn't scare me. We will meet trickery with trickery. I will go dressed as a rich young foreigner with a bushy beard and the Hoghigs shall go with me as my pageboys and I

shall shoot for this golden arrow and
if we win it we will hang it in the great hollow oak."

Nottingham Town looked grand on the day of the
shooting match, with bright flags flying and rows of
benches set out for the wealthy businessmen of the
city and their families.

Near the target was a raised seat bedecked with
ribbons and scarves and garlands of flowers. The
Sheriff of Nottingham would sit there with his
beady-eyed wife, Lady Rosabella.

At the other side of the shooting range was a
fence to keep poor people from crowding in front
of the target. Already the place was filling up
with excited men, women, children and animals.

In a special tent of striped canvas, the archers
gathered in twos and threes. Some boasted loudly
to fellow marksmen. Others silently inspected their
bowstrings and arrows for any faults. Many of the
best archers in England had come to Nottingham
for the match.

The Sheriff rode up with his lady. He was in fine
purple velvet with golden chains. She wore a blue
velvet gown trimmed with swansdown and carried
a monkey on a silver chain. They dismounted,
to be greeted by the cheers of men-at-arms in
yellow uniform who waved their spears in salute.

The Sheriff and his wife sat down. The Sheriff gave a
signal. Silver trumpets sang. The archers stepped forward to
their places. Everybody began to shout, many of them calling
out the name of their favourite: "Red Cap!", "Cruikshank!" or
"Hey for Adam of the Dell!" All the ladies waved their scarves.

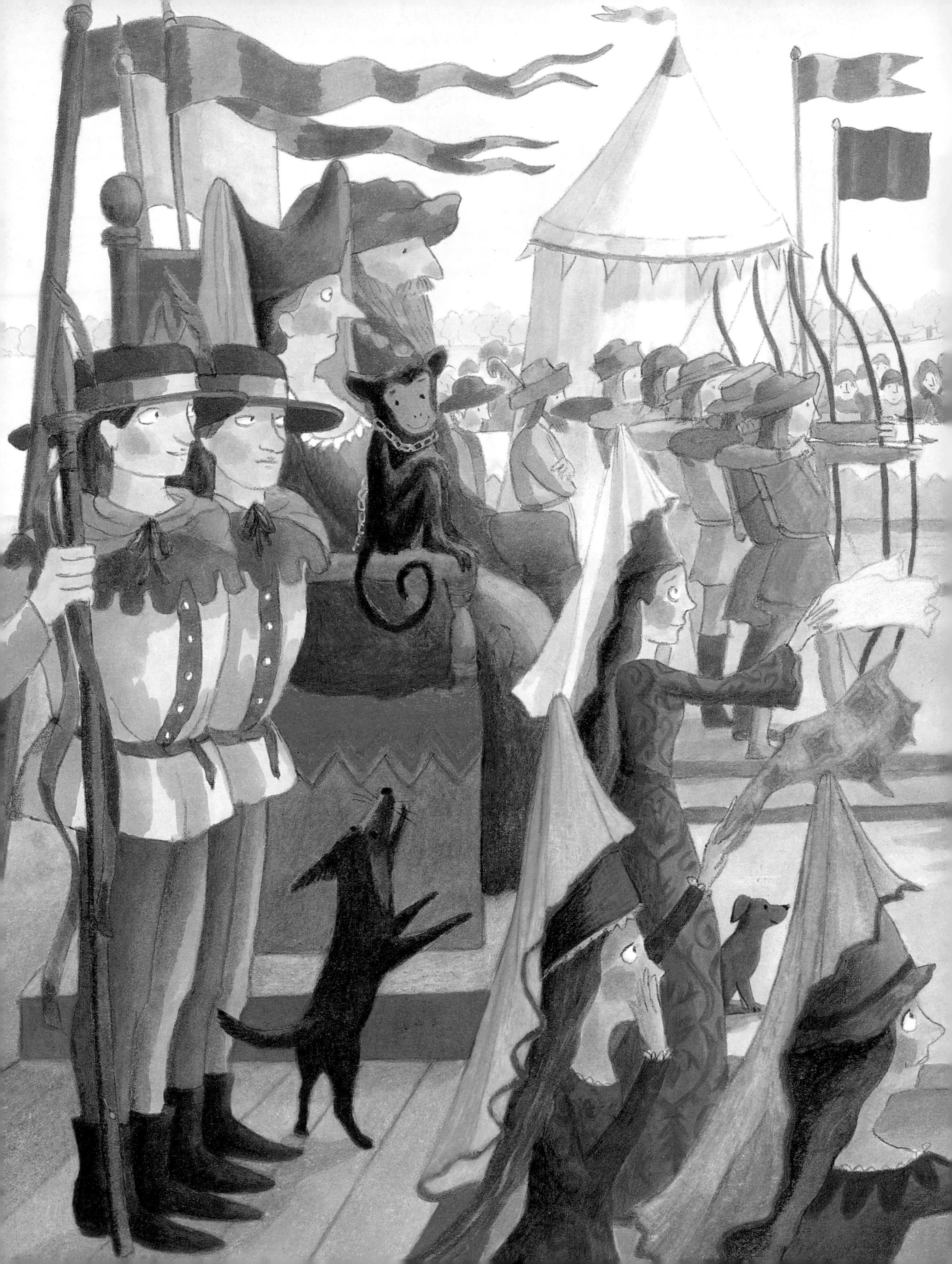

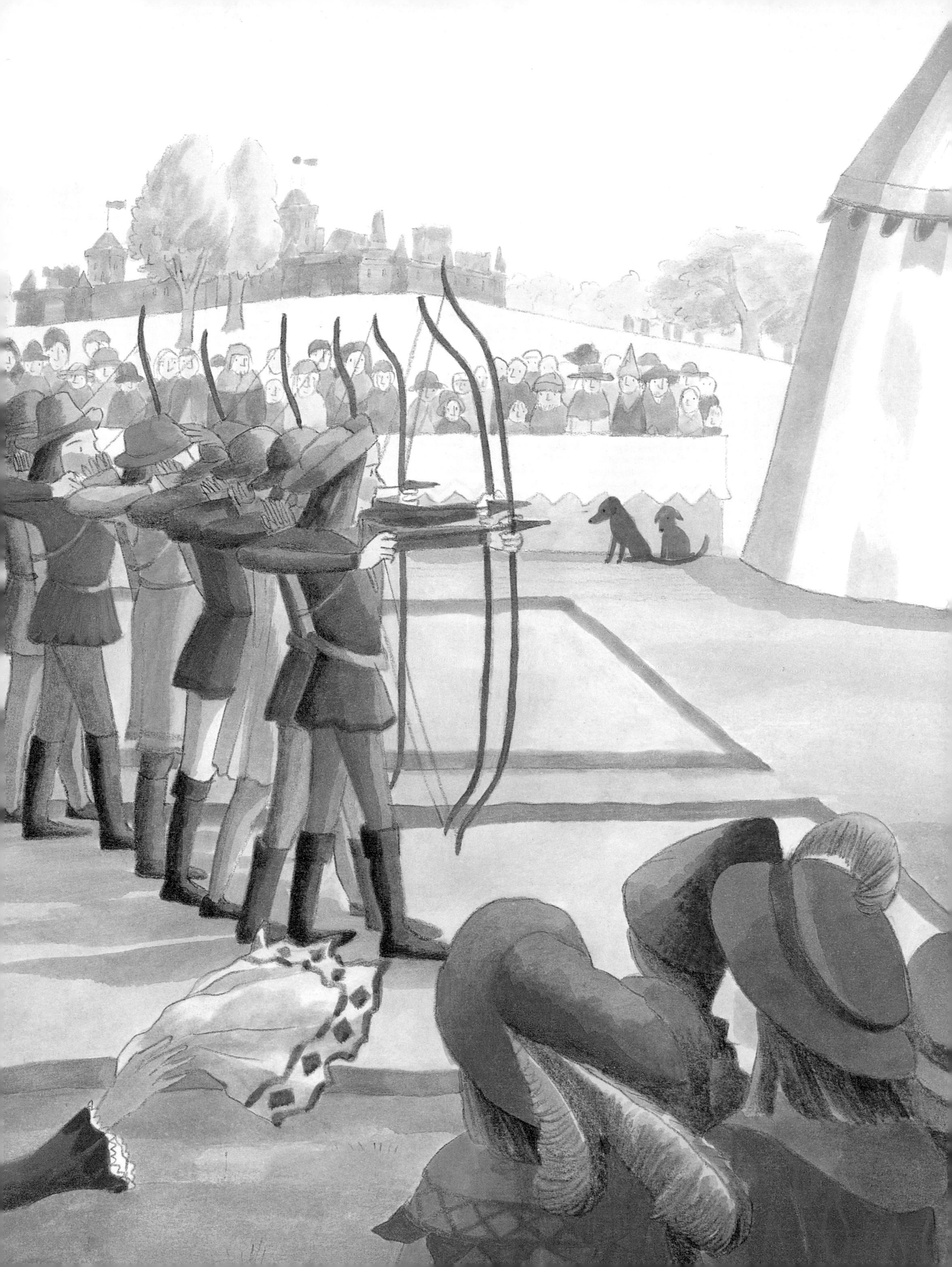

The Sheriff leaned forward, looking keenly into the crowd of archers to see if he could find Robin Hood. There was nobody dressed in the Lincoln green Robin always wore, but it was a knock-out contest and the Sheriff was sure that when the mob of marksmen was reduced to ten or fewer he would be able to spot his enemy.

The archers shot and that day it was great shooting. The people shouted, for they had never seen such marksmanship. Soon there were only eight left in the match.

Among them were some famous archers: Gill of the Red Cap – the Sheriff's chief archer – Adam of the Dell, Diccon Cruikshank, William of Leslie, Hubert of Cloud and Swithin of Hertford. There were two unknown contenders. One was a tall man in blue who said he came from London. The other was a wealthy-looking stranger in scarlet who wore a bushy black beard and was accompanied by two black pageboys in scarlet livery.

The Sheriff turned to Sir Ralph, who crouched beside his chair. "Can you see Robin Hood?" asked the Sheriff.

"I don't think so," said Sir Ralph. "I know most of them well, being a betting man. Perhaps the man in blue? I don't know. I think Robin Hood is a coward as well as a villain and hasn't dared to show his face."

The eight men stepped forward to shoot again. Each archer shot two arrows and all were near the centre of the target. The judges took some time to choose the three finalists: Gill of the Red Cap, Adam of the Dell and the wealthy-looking stranger in scarlet.

"Shoot well, Gill," shouted the Sheriff. "If yours is the best shaft I'll give you a hundred silver pennies as well as the prize."

"I'll do my best," said Gill sturdily. He drew his bow with

care and sped the shaft. It stuck in the target, only the breadth of a finger from the centre. "Gill! Gill!" shouted all the crowd, and the Sheriff clapped and smiled.

Adam of the Dell shot cautiously. His shot was good, but not good enough, so he retired, graciously.

The stranger in scarlet walked up. A pageboy handed him an arrow, which he fitted to his bow. He stood quite still while you could count to five.

Nobody breathed.

The arrow flew straight and so truly that it knocked a grey goose feather off Gill's shaft. That feather fell fluttering through the sunlit air. The stranger's arrow lodged in the dead centre of the target.

For a moment nobody spoke and nobody shouted, but everyone stared at the stranger in scarlet with the bushy black beard. (Everybody except the Sheriff's beady-eyed wife, Lady Rosabella, who had been bitten on the nose by her monkey.)

The Sheriff held out to the winner the priceless golden arrow, gleaming wonderfully, alive with light.

"Here, my good man," said the Sheriff. "Take your prize, for you have won it fairly. What is your name, and where do you come from?"

"I am the Duke of Ecalpon," said the man in scarlet in a strange accent which sounded like a bear with a sore throat, "and I am from the land of Twon."

The Sheriff bowed his head and smiled. Then, hoping to win some popularity, he turned to the crowd. "Let us salute our noble visitor," he cried. "Long Live the Duke of Ecalpon! Long live the great land of Twon!"

All the people echoed the Sheriff's shout and the Duke, holding on to his bushy beard with one hand, raised the golden arrow high in the air to the applause of the crowd. Then, with his two pageboys, he marched from the scene of his triumph as the scarves waved and the people shouted their acclaim.

Under the great hollow oak that night the outlaws celebrated loud and long as Robin sat on a couch of moss beside Marian, underneath a branch from which hung the golden arrow. Alan A-Dale sang a great ballad of the archery contest and the Hoghigs danced till they fell down.

That same night, at dinner in his great hall, the Sheriff

turned thoughtfully to Sir Ralph. "I could have sworn," he said, "that Robin would be at the contest. I never thought him such a coward. Without him there, Gill should surely have won. And he would have, if it hadn't been for the Duke of Ecalpon, from the land of Twon."

As he spoke, there was a faint whistle and something fell rattling among the dishes on the table. The Sheriff's wife, who wore a dainty bandage on her nose, picked it up. Everyone at table saw what it was – a blunted grey goose arrow with a fine scroll tied near its head.

Lady Rosabella opened the scroll and read its message slowly:

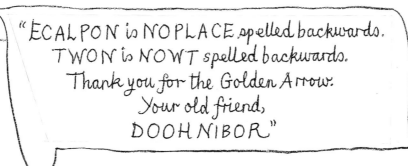

"ECALPON is NO PLACE spelled backwards.
TWON is NOWT spelled backwards.
Thank you for the Golden Arrow.
Your old friend,
DOOH NIBOR"

The New Friar

"Happy birthday, Father!"

It was Baron Fitzwater's forty-fifth or fifty-fourth birthday. He smiled at his daughter Lady Matilda with all his fifteen good teeth.

She wore a robe of crimson, his favourite colour, with wild white roses in her midnight-coloured hair. She gave him a kiss on the cheek and ruffled his hair.

He was a very happy old Baron as he unrolled her present. It was a tapestry she had specially embroidered for him, the work of many moons. It showed a gallant castle with a fine nobleman standing on one turret, bearing a sword and an emblazoned shield. With a glad leap in the heart the Baron realised that the castle was his castle and he himself was that fine nobleman.

He gazed at the delicate details of the tapestry-work – the meadow in which you could see every blade of grass and count the star-like daisies. There were rabbits bounding through the grass – to the Baron they looked good enough to eat.

Baron Fitzwater sighed as he unrolled some more of the

54

tapestry and saw – what was this? – she had also carefully embroidered the picture of that infernal forest.

"It's not fair," he bellowed. "Why give me a picture of Sherwood Forest when you know it upsets me?"

"I thought that if I showed you how beautiful the forest is you might grow to love it."

"How can a Baron love a forest? A forest is just a clump of timber full of criminals."

"Robin Hood is no criminal, Father!"

"How dare you! Bob Locksley is an outlaw and I won't have him named at my table. Go to your room at once."

"I shall go, sir, but not to my room."

"Not to your room? I order you to your room, girl."

"I am a grown woman – and I shall go wherever I choose," said Lady Matilda and as she strode from the hall it was obvious she was changing into Maid Marian and making for her beloved forest.

The Baron's birthday was ruined – almost. Almost, but not quite, for he suddenly remembered his birthday treat. Friar Michael had promised to cook him an Arlington Pasty.

Now an Arlington Pasty was the invention of the Friar. It was about twice the size of your head. It was a bulging envelope of munchy golden pastry containing every single good and tasty thing your tongue and stomach could desire. Once a year it was cooked, by order of the Baron. It would be served by Friar Michael in half an hour. The Baron drummed his hands on his empty stomach and smiled.

At that very moment the Friar was taking the pasty from the great oven and hauling it on to the stone table to cool. Clouds of sweet steam rose towards the ceiling.

"By the deep purple eyes of Saint Storella, you are indeed a beautiful pasty. And by the enormous nostrils of Saint Barnaby, you smell like a masterpiece of piecraft."

The Friar waddled around the giant pasty, singing

quietly to himself or perhaps to the pie. Then an awful thought struck him.

"Suppose," he said to himself, "just suppose that those unusual mushrooms I plucked this morning, the ones with the purple spots, were really poisonous toadstools and that they are even now spreading their venom throughout the mighty pasty and that when the Baron demolishes his birthday treat those toadstools do twist his innards into reef-knots – what then? I will be hanged as a naughty Friar. And then who will look after my excellent cat and my two fine hairy dogs?"

So it was because of his love of animals that the Friar persuaded himself that he should take just one taste of the pasty. And then another. And another.

Twenty minutes later Friar Michael found that he was sharing the last crumbs of the Baron's birthday pasty with his dogs Hayrick and Stubbs and his cat Helena. Twenty-five minutes later, they were awoken by a terrible crackling sound.

It was the birthday Baron wielding a nasty little whip. He chased them out of the kitchen, out of the castle, out of Arlington, shouting out oaths which are always kept out of books, and the Friar ran until he was out of sight, out of breath and, most definitely, out of a job. With his animals at his heels, he slouched towards Sherwood Forest.

He was just approaching the river which separates Arlington from Sherwood when he met Robin Hood, who wore a fine suit of Lincoln green and a slim sword at his side. The two men had only met once – at the interrupted wedding – so they nodded to each other.

Robin decided he must prove who was the master. The nearest way to cross the river was by the ford, a shallow patch of river that was only about knee-deep at this time of year.

"You see this ford," he said to the Friar. "You know I'd very much like to cross it. But as you see, I am wearing my finest clothes and they would spoil in the water. You have broad shoulders, do you think you could find it in your heart to carry me across?"

"Now by the blue big toe of Saint Monica," blustered the Friar in a rage, "do you – you kiss-in-the-ring popinjay – ask me, the holy Brother Michael, to carry you through the water?" Then an idea came to him, his eyes twinkled and he changed his tone. "And yet, why shouldn't I carry you? Did not Saint Christopher himself carry a mysterious child over the river? Come, friend, climb on my back."

The white-masked black cat, Helena, leapt on top of the

Friar's head. Then a thought occurred to Friar Michael and he said: "Good Robin Hood, let me carry your fine sword under my arm so that its blade is kept from the water."

Robin handed over his sword in its scabbard. The Friar clenched it under his armpit and bent again to let Robin climb aboard.

The Friar was small, but very sturdy, and he carried Robin across the ford safely enough, Hayrick and Stubbs swimming along behind him doggedly.

Robin jumped lightly from the Friar's broad back.

"Many thanks," he said. "You are a good and holy man. Now please give me back my sword, for I must be on my way to meet Maid Marian."

The Friar looked at Robin for a long time and then slowly winked his right eye.

"Oh, no," he said gently. "You may be in a hurry, but I have business too – on the other side of the stream. I have humbly obeyed you. Now it is your turn. You will observe that I have a sword in my hand and you have none. So be persuaded, by the bloody battle axe of Saint Botulph, to carry me back again."

Robin had no choice. He bent down and let the Friar leap on to his back. It was like carrying a sack of soft rocks.

Robin had never crossed this particular ford before, so that he stumbled over stones, stepped into deep holes and nearly tripped over a boulder. Meanwhile the Friar dug his heels into Robin's sides and shouted at him to gee-up as if he were a stubborn donkey.

By the time they reached the far side and the Friar slipped down, Robin was soaked to the shoulders. But he wasn't finished. He blew on his bugle-horn three times to summon his men. Then he knocked the sword out of the Friar's hand, caught it by the handle and pointed it at him.

"All right, you holy trickster, now carry me back across the ford or I will turn you into a sieve with this sharp sword."

"Oh, dear," said the Friar. "I do dislike violence. But since you have called for a battle, you shall have a war." The Friar whistled three times.

Helena the cat, who was perched on the Friar's shoulder, leapt and landed on Robin's head. She clutched the back of his scalp with her back paws and began to scratch at his forehead with her front claws.

Help was at hand. Little John and Will Scarlett came stamping through the waters of the ford. But before they could reach Robin, who was struggling to disentangle himself from the cat while the Friar was kicking him from behind, two hairy thunderbolts – Hayrick and Stubbs – hurtled at their ankles and sent them sprawling into the river.

It was a ridiculous fight and it ended in laughter. Robin had certainly lost the fight – he carried those cat-scratch scars for the rest of his days and he couldn't sit down for a week – but he gained a friend. For the Friar called off his three brave animals and the men shook hands all round.

Robin laughed. "Good Friar Michael, will you and your creatures come and join me and my band of outlaws in the forest?"

"That was my very intention when I walked this way," said the Friar, "for I have been the tutor to Maid Marian since she was a little girl and she has told me much about you and your forest games."

"Then you must take a new name," said Robin, "for we all take new names when we come to live in Sherwood."

The four men and three animals walked together in silence for some time. As they came in sight of the outlaws' camp, the Friar stopped.

"I would like to be called by the name of Friar Tuck," he said. "And this very night, by the huge hips of Saint Dolores, I shall cook for all of you a Sherwood Pasty."

His eyes brightened as he saw the smoke from a good fire and Marian, in her scarlet robe, running to greet him.

"Yes," he said, "I will be Friar Tuck."

Raining in Sherwood

"Move over, by the icy belly of Saint Bowlby. There's great blobs of wet dropping on my head," moaned Friar Tuck.

"Serves you right for being bald," said Will Scarlett, and got a mighty elbow in the ribs as his reward.

It was raining in Sherwood. It had been raining for weeks, but this was the thickest, chilliest rain anyone could remember. The outlaws were huddled around Robin's great oak tree. The Hoghigs curled up inside its hollow trunk. Even there the rain flowed down. They might as well have been sitting underneath a waterfall.

"Everything's soaking," grumbled Little John. "Our clothes, our shoes, our bedding. Our arrow feathers are so wet they won't fly. They'll only be good for shooting fish and rabbits in their burrows."

"You're a bright lad, Little John," said Will Scarlett.

"This isn't normal rain," said Robin. "It's like a second deluge. Maybe we ought to build a Noah's ark and start collecting animals, two of each – "

"Well, there's two asses here," said Much the Miller's son, pulling the ears of the Hoghigs. Robin wasn't pleased.

"Will you all stop teasing each other?"
he said. "We've been a whole year in the woods together.
And we're all cold and we're all wet through – "

"*And we're fed up with the forest*
Fed up with the forest – "
sang Alan A-Dale, but Robin glowered at him so fiercely that
he stopped in mid-quaver.

"Don't moan," said Robin. "The best thing is not to think
about being wet. From now on, any outlaw who talks about
the rain takes a thump on the head from Friar Tuck."

"What else is there to talk about?" asked Little John, who
was great in a fight but not so good at conversation.

"What are we going to call ourselves?" said Robin. "Now
that's a good subject for intelligent discussion."

"How can we be intelligent under water?" asked Will
Scarlett, then remembered and held out his head meekly for
a buffet from the Friar.

"Every other gang I ever heard of had a name," said Robin.
"I've heard of the Briarwood Lads and the Deadly Boys and
the Roarers and the Patcheyes."

"We could be the Holy Fools," said Friar Tuck.
"Or God's Own Robbers."

"No," said Will Scarlett. "That's too churchy. Let's be
the Lightnings."

"Don't let's have anything about weather," said Little John.

"We want to sound scary. How about the Grisly Ghosts of Sherwood Forest?"

"Far too long," said Will Scarlett. "Why not the Thousand Ghouls?"

"'Cos there aren't a thousand of us, stupid," said Little John. "Not nearly."

"It's to scare people – it doesn't have to be true," said Scarlett.

Much the Miller's son spoke up: "Why can't we be the Friends of Marian?"

"Because that's soft," said Robin contemptuously. "Can you imagine the Sheriff of Nottingham's thugs shivering in their armour in case they met the Friends of Marian? No, we want something brave. Why can't we be the Arrows of Justice?"

"Because it sounds wet – like we are," said Little John, then fell into a scrum of a wrestling match with all the others as he refused to let Friar Tuck thump him for mentioning the rain. They were tumbling all over each other, using knees and elbows and feet and churning up a ton of leaves and mud, when they heard a tooting sound through the trees. They staggered to their feet.

At the far end of a silver-dripping path stood Marian blowing a bugle. The outlaws walked towards her and saw, to their astonishment, that a great tent had been raised in a clearing.

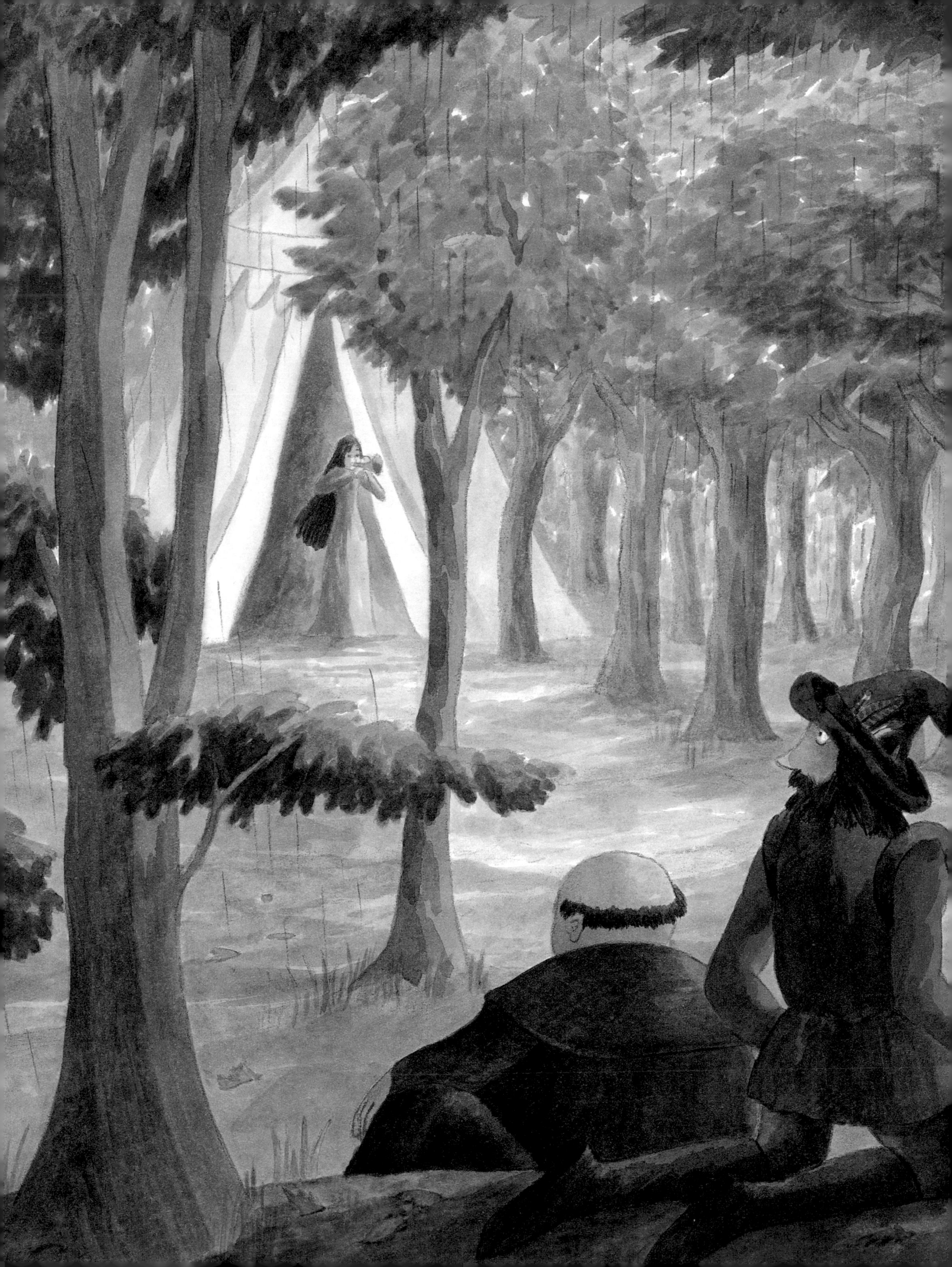

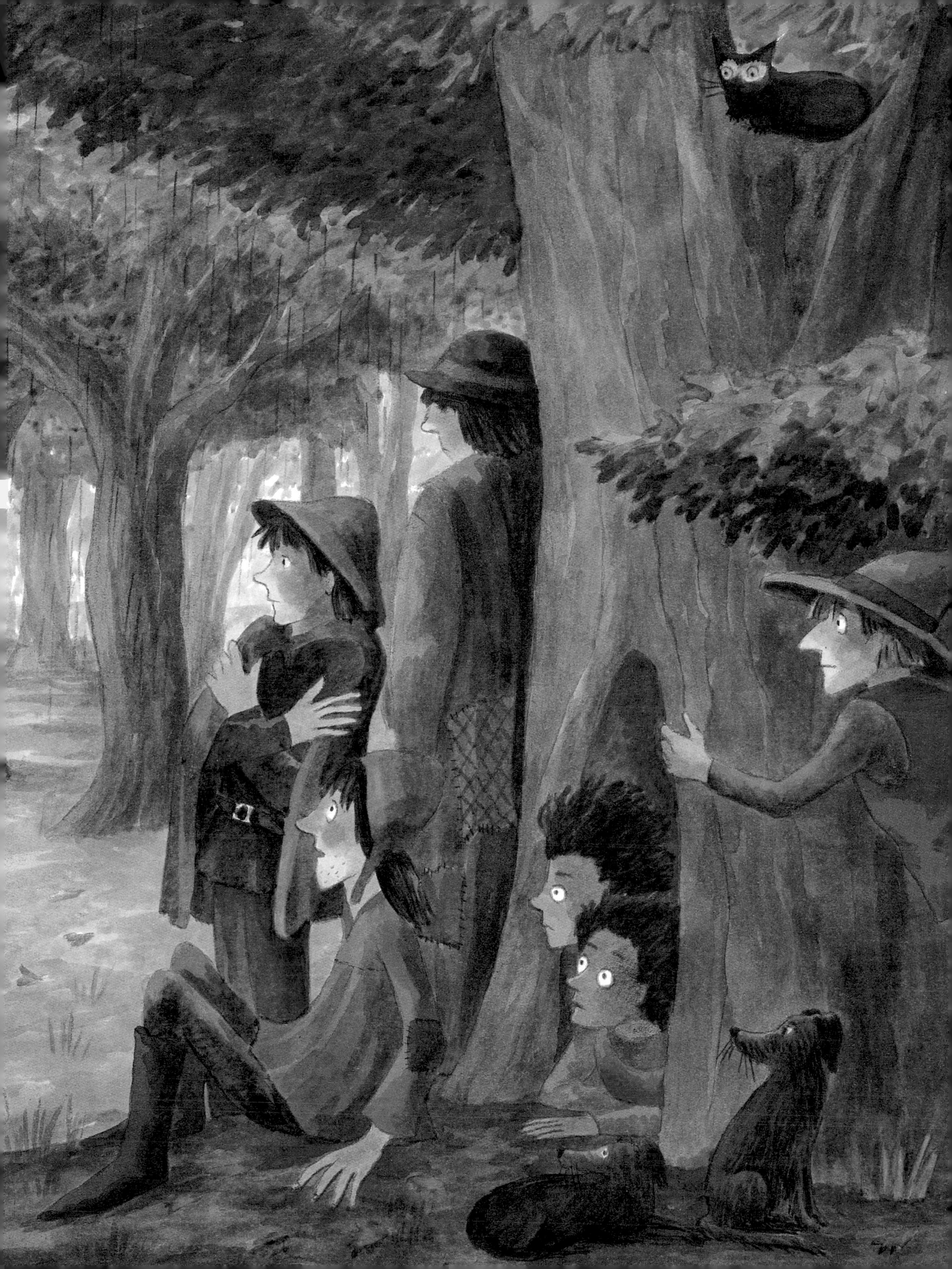

Marian welcomed them into the dryness. There were red-burning braziers to warm up freezing hands and bodies. Hundreds of little candles were crowned with golden flames.

And there, on a wooden table, stood the biggest cake any outlaw ever dreamed about. It bore one great candle. And on that cake were written these words: *For Robin Hood and his Merry Men.*

"It's a beautiful cake," said Much the Miller's son, wiping a tear from the corner of his eye.

Marian produced a sword and handed it to Robin, who cut the cake carefully, making a secret wish. Nobody spoke until the whole cake had been cut and munched and washed down with perry, the cider which is made from pears.

"Why did you decide to call us the Merry Men?" asked Little John.

"Because you're never grumpy," said Marian, wickedly. "Look – now the sun's come back."

And indeed, when they looked out of the tent, all they could see was golden light shining from the green and brown wetness of the forest and a clean-washed blue sky overhead.

"It's a day for adventures," said Robin.

But the big man still wasn't happy.

"I've been living out here in this wet and windy forest just as long as Robin," complained Little John. "Why aren't I on the cake? Why doesn't it say Robin Hood and Little John and their Merry Men? I suppose it was because you ran out of cake, was it?"

"We're not on the cake either," said Jemmy.

"But we're not complaining," said Jenny.

"We can't all be on the cake," said the Hoghigs.

Marian spoke quietly but firmly. "It says Robin, because

Robin is our leader and Robin is the most dangerous outlaw in the forest. Look here." She unrolled a scroll and read it aloud. "*Dead or Alive. I do offer the reward of 40 golden crowns for the notorious outlaw Robin Hood. And I do offer five golden crowns for each member of his gang of ruffians, most especially Will Scarlett, Much the Miller's son and Little Jack. Signed, Maurice Marre, Sheriff of Nottingham.*"

Little John's face became a thundercloud. "Little Jack? All right," he said. "I'll show him who's the most dangerous outlaw in Sherwood. Out of my way."

Picking up his quarterstaff, Little John strode out of the tent, splashing along the path which led to Nottingham. "They couldn't even get my name right," he muttered as he beheaded a wild rose with his staff.

"He's looking for the worst kind of trouble," said Marian. "Jenny and Jemmy, you'd better follow him. Keep your distance, but make sure nothing happens to him."

Pausing only to scoop up a handful of cakecrumbs each, the Hoghigs were on their way.

Hours passed in talk and shooting practice and cooking and the drying of green clothes. The sun set. The moon rose. The outlaws sat around a crackling fire. Alan A-Dale was singing:

"The Merry Men were down at heart
So Marian did bake
And put one birthday candle on
A famous birthday cake.

And the Merry Men then made merry
As they ate mighty slices of cake.
They scoffed every currant and every cherry – "

Suddenly the Hoghig twins, all splashed with mud and wild of eye, were standing by the fire, shouting:
"Dozens of soldiers – "
"All in armour – "
"Riding on horses – "
"Huge great swords – "
"Little John went for them – "
"Knocked two of them off their horses – "
"But they battered him to the ground – "
"Tied him up in a net – "

"And they dragged him off behind a horse."

The anger was rising in Robin.

"Where did they take him?"

"They were the Sheriff's men," said Jenny.

"They've tooken him to Nottingham Castle," said Jemmy.

"It's my fault," said Robin. "I shouldn't have let him stamp off in such a temper."

"We'll all go and rescue him," said Will Scarlett.

"Yes, by the purple beard of Saint Macintosh!"

"No," said Robin. "Just me. They'll have him in the castle by now. Probably they've dropped him down that Bottle Dungeon. There's only a dozen of us and the Sheriff's got hundreds of soldiers. Cunning's the only way to rescue Little John. One spy may enter where an army cannot. Bring my old man's disguise."

The Hoghigs brought Robin's grey wig and spectacles and his robe of tatters and he pulled on the clothes over his Lincoln green.

"They'll torture you, Robin. They'll hang you up in chains –" said Marian.

"First of all they'll have to catch me," said Robin with a nervous grin. "If they do, well, you may all come and rescue me. Till then – stay here in the greenwood – and be merry."

Robin chose a rugged old staff and headed off down the path that Little John had followed. After a few miles he came to a crossing of the paths and decided to take the short cut through Boggarts' Swamp. This was a place of broken tree stumps rising from dark bogpools. It was ghostly enough by day. Now, lit by the moon, its mists swirled like silver phantoms dancing. There was a stench of graveyards in the air. The path was hard to follow. In many places it was ankle deep in muddy water.

He stepped on to a small dryish island in the swamp and sat down with his back to an old weeping willow. Carefully he emptied the water from his shoes. An owl hooted. Robin thought of Little John in that cold, dark, stony dungeon.

Suddenly he felt he was not alone on the island. Silently he stood and moved round the willow. He found a grey mare tethered to a branch and, standing beside it, a strange, large man.

Robin had never seen anything like him. From head to foot he was clothed in the hide of a horse, with the dark hairs still on it. On his head was a hood of the same stuff, with ears sticking up like a rabbit. There were slit-holes for his eyes, but the hood concealed all of his face except his mouth. By his side hung a heavy broadsword and a slim, double-edged dagger. A quiver of arrows hung on his shoulder and his longbow leaned against the tree.

"Hello, my friend," said Robin, remembering to speak like the old man he was pretending to be, "what's that hairy suit you're wearing? Are you to act in a nativity play? The part of a camel, perhaps? Or are you a messenger from Old Nick, come to call me down to an appointment in hell?"

The stranger pushed up the hood an inch or two, and Robin could see that he sported a yellow moustache above his thin, cruel mouth.

"I wear this horse's skin, you fool, to keep my body warm as I go hunting through the forest. And it will be nearly as good as steel armour against the sword of my enemy." The man pulled back his hood. Robin saw those burning blue eyes and that mane of yellow hair.

"As for my name, it is Sir Ralph Montfalcon. You may have heard of me." Robin nodded wisely. "The Sheriff of Nottingham has offered forty crowns for the capture of Robin Hood. And I have sworn not to leave Sherwood Forest until I have hunted down that scurvy outlaw and delivered him, dead or alive, to the Sheriff."

Robin kept his temper and still spoke as an old man. "I know this Robin Hood very well, and I think he may prove to be the better man."

Sir Ralph laughed loud and long. "Hood is a petty

criminal – without his gang of cut-throats he is nothing. Why, I broke up his wedding single-handed and he ran away. And when he is dead I will marry the lady he stole away, the beautiful Lady Matilda Fitzwater. If Hood stood before me in combat, I would cut him down within ten seconds. I hear that he has never killed a man in all his life. Some call him a great archer, but I could outshoot him any day of the year."

Robin was by now shaking with anger, but he still pretended to be an old man. "Truly," he said, "they do call Robin a great archer, but we are all good with the longbow in Sherwood. I may be old, but I would happily chance a bout against you."

"You would shoot? With my bow?" asked Sir Ralph.

Robin nodded in an ancient way. "Yes," he said, "and I would wager two gold crowns that I could outshoot you."

"Done!" exclaimed Sir Ralph. "Three arrows each at a target. The nearest arrow to take the prize."

"Done!" Robin nodded and each man placed two shining golden coins on a tree stump.

"These will do for a target," said Sir Ralph, pulling off Robin's spectacles. He measured out a hundred paces and tied the glasses to the branch of a tree, then rejoined Robin by the willow. "Three arrows each."

Sir Ralph shot first. His first arrow overshot the fork. But his second and third lodged in the branch, two inches either side of the spectacles.

Robin, still in the role of an old man, pretended to have great difficulty drawing back the string of Sir Ralph's bow and let his first arrow shoot into the ground. Sir Ralph laughed like a hyena, but his laughter suddenly faded.

Robin's second arrow broke the left-hand lens of the spectacles. His third broke the right-hand lens. Robin pocketed the four gold coins. Then he dropped the bow and flung his disguise to the ground. He reached slowly for his sword.

"That shows how much you know about sport," said Robin. "Now we shall see how well you can fight. Today, Sir Ralph, I think you will yield to a better man – for I am Robin Hood." His sword flashed into the sunlight and he gave his other smile – the dangerous one.

Sir Ralph stared for a moment. Then he was overcome with rage. "I'm glad to meet you, and even gladder to send you on a speedy journey to hell."

There followed the most ferocious fight ever seen in Sherwood. Robin knew he could expect no mercy. They fought up and down, till all the sweet green grass was crushed and ground under their heels. Both men took flesh wounds and their blood sprinkled over the moss of the forest floor.

At last Sir Ralph made a desperate lunge at Robin. Robin stepped backwards, caught his heel on a root and fell upon his back. Sir Ralph stood astride him, but as he stabbed downwards, Robin caught the blade in his bare hand and, though it cut his palm, he turned the point away so that it plunged deep into the ground.

Before another blow could be struck, Robin was on his feet, confronting Sir Ralph, now only armed with his dagger. Robin suddenly noticed something. The white glove on Sir Ralph's left hand had been ripped off in the fight.

That hand bore on one finger a gold ring in the shape of a serpent. And across the back of that pink hand were the white scars of ten small teeth, with a gap between them.

Robin remembered what Marian had told him. This was the murderer of his own father. Red anger rose from his heart and he could hardly see his enemy. He slashed out with the flat of his sword.

Sir Ralph staggered backwards. He felt his feet being dragged from under him. The whole world seemed to be pulling him horribly downwards. He was being sucked into the dark belly of the swamp.

As the hungry mud reached his waist, he began to shout for help. Robin watched him. The dark mud pulled at his chest, then his shoulders. Sir Ralph started screaming. Robin did nothing. He was remembering his father and he was thinking of Marian.

Sir Ralph's head was swallowed by the swamp and finally only one hand, with its golden snake ring, was above the deadly surface.

After a while Robin tied a rope around that hand's wrist, tied the other end of the rope to Sir Ralph's horse, and pulled the mud-covered corpse out of the bog.

Robin drew off the horse-hide clothes and put his own Lincoln green on Sir Ralph's body. The dead man's face was so thick with mud that it was unrecognisable, but Robin used Sir Ralph's dagger to shave off the moustache, just in case, then covered the upper lip with a fresh coat of mud.

He hoisted up the corpse and tied it behind the saddle of Sir Ralph's horse. He washed the worst of the mud off the horse-hide clothes and put them on. Their hood gave him a very effective mask.

Robin hid his old-man disguise in the fork of the tree in case he ever needed it again. Then he untied the grey mare and began to ride it towards the Sheriff's castle. Not too fast – he didn't want to arrive before dark.

The Bottle Dungeon

The Sheriff stroked his reddish beard, which was always a sign of trouble for somebody. That somebody was Little John, who stood before him, glaring, but safely entangled in a strong fishing net held by four burly armed men.

"I'm so glad you called, Little John," said the Sheriff. "I would like to welcome you to my special guest room. We call it – the Bottle Dungeon."

"What's that, Porridgeface?" asked Little John

"It won't help you to be rude," said the Sheriff. "The Bottle Dungeon has been especially prepared for you and other forest rats. Imagine a bottle which has been buried upright in a hole in the ground, with only an inch or two of the neck showing above ground level. Now imagine that the bottle is made out of smooth stone. The piece of neck above the ground is like the wall around a well.

"The guest is lowered down to the bottom of the bottle like a bucket into a well. And left there. He can't climb out. And nobody climbs down. Stale bread and stagnant water are lowered down to him once a day, in silence.

78

"Down in the Bottle Dungeon it is completely dark for twenty-four hours a day. So the guest gradually goes blind. There is also complete silence and a great loneliness and lack of hope down in the Bottle Dungeon. So the guest gradually goes mad."

"Which comes first, the blindness or the madness?" asked Little John.

"I never worried about that," said the Sheriff. "But I'm sure you'll soon find out." The Sheriff stood up, walked over to Little John and spat in his eye for luck. "Lower him down."

So the big man, like a writhing dolphin in a net, was lowered down into the pitch dark. Once he bumped against the stone floor of his night-filled cell it didn't take him long to tear off the net. He folded it up to form some kind of mattress. The rope which had lowered him was cranked up. Little John sat down on his net. He was alone in the dark silence. He whistled a springtime tune. At least there was a good echo.

Then he heard a scratching sound. Little John felt something he had not felt for years – fear. It was as if a great icicle had pierced his stomach. Then came a whimpering in the dark. What had they done? Had they lowered a baby into this little hell?

More whimpering – some lonely and frightened creature. Pity overcame fear. Little John made little low crooning noises. He stretched out a hand towards the creature and touched a bunch of hair. Fur? Whatever this being was, he would try to console his fellow prisoner. Little John took the thing he could not see in both his great hands and held it to his chest, gently but firmly. He could feel the wild beating of its small heart. He stroked the creature's hairy back, its long, stringy tail. He touched its round furry head and realised that it must be a monkey, yes, the monkey famous for biting Lady Rosabella's nose. It was paying cruelly for that crime.

Little John was glad to have company. He hummed the tune of an old song and danced slowly in the darkness with the little monkey in his arms.

The Sheriff dined well that night, and so did his men. They celebrated the capture of Little John with flagon after flagon of rough red wine. They were beginning to yawn when a sentry ushered a strange figure into the hall, ghastly in the light of flickering torches.

It wore the mud-covered, horse-hide clothes of Sir Ralph Montfalcon. But under the masking hood with its silly rabbit's ears was the watchful face of Robin Hood.

The Sheriff called out: "It's Sir Ralph, by all that's wonderful! Come, sit down, join us in a glass and tell us what has happened to you in Sherwood. Why, man, you're all covered in mud."

"Forgive me, Sheriff, I've not taken the time to change or bathe. For I have come straight from drowning in the swamp the vilest creature who ever crawled through the forest."

"Sir Ralph, if that's true, this is the best day of your life."

Robin kept his voice low and harsh, like the voice of his dead enemy. "Of course it's true," he said. "Look, isn't this Robin Hood's sword? Isn't this his longbow?"

"But where's his body?" asked the Sheriff. Robin clicked his fingers and two of the Sheriff's servants dragged along the stone floor of the hall the body of Sir Ralph dressed in Robin's clothes of Lincoln green.

The Sheriff drained another goblet of wine, then peered at the corpse. It could have been anybody's face under all that mud, but the Sheriff badly wanted to see Robin Hood dead. So that is what he saw.

Then he laughed and clapped his hands. "What a great day! The terrible outlaw is dead and I have Little John, his second-in-command, imprisoned in my Bottle Dungeon. The forty gold crowns are yours, Sir Ralph!"

"I enjoyed killing that thief," said Robin in his Sir Ralphish voice, "and so I want no money. Just give me Little John and let me give him his deserts." Robin stroked his sword meanly.

"You're a fool to pass up that money," said the Sheriff. "And I'm sorry to give up that big oaf – I'd planned a dozen special torments for him before he died. But the favour you have done me and all in England in drowning Robin Hood forces me to grant your wish. Fetch up Little John!"

The big man had been sleeping, but he was glad to be hauled out of his stone bottle, with the monkey inside his shirt. But he wasn't so pleased to confront this man with muddy clothes and rabbit's ears. The Sheriff introduced him with mock courtesy.

"Little John, I'd like you to meet Sir Ralph Montfalcon, who has this day drowned in the slime of a swamp that notorious outlaw Robin Hood."

Little John struggled, but his arms were bound in front of him and four yellow-coated men held him. Two daggers pointed at his great throat as the big fellow shouted: "You cowardly villain. Robin had the gentlest heart that ever beat in England. If Robin is dead, then I will die too, and I don't care how." The salt tears rolled down Little John's brown cheeks.

"Thanks for giving me this prisoner," said Robin to the Sheriff. "Now, men, hold him against that wall and let me show you how we stick a pig where I come from."

Two of the Sheriff's men shook their heads when they heard this. They didn't care if Little John was forgotten in a dungeon. But they didn't like to see a man butchered in cold blood. But the Sheriff shouted at them, ordering them to hold the man still.

Robin walked forward. His sword slashed the ropes that bound Little John, and suddenly the big man was free, with Robin's good sword in one hand, the other clutching the monkey inside his shirt. And Robin was at his side, his longbow ready to fire a shining arrow through anyone who dared attack.

The Sheriff's soldiers retreated towards the door and out into the night. Robin threw back the stupid hood with its rabbit's ears. That dangerous smile spread slowly across his face. Then the Sheriff knew that Robin Hood was back from the dead.

The Sheriff turned and ran down a draughty corridor hung with scarlet tapestries, through a doorway carved with cherubs, down a spiral staircase and into a huge unlit room. All the way the footsteps of Robin and Little John followed him.

The Sheriff crouched in the blackness. Hide-and-seek in the dark, he thought. I'll give them the slip. But the dark vanished as Little John and Robin marched into the room holding blazing torches. The Sheriff raised his arm across his eyes and staggered backwards. And backwards.

Too late he realised that he was somersaulting back over a small stone wall like the wall around a well. Too late he realised that he was falling like a great stone into the total darkness of his own Bottle Dungeon. His scream, as he fell, echoed horribly. Then the scream stopped. The Bottle Dungeon was filled with the silence of death.

As they left the castle, Robin and Little John touched their burning torches to every tapestry they passed. By the time they were a mile away the whole castle was ablaze.

It was midnight. As they walked towards the forest Little John thought how good it was to be out in the open air again. The night breeze tickled his face. A thousand stars were out to welcome him back to freedom. The small monkey perched on his shoulder, chattering happily. The moon laughed, and so did Little John.

King Robin, Queen Marian

It was a hot, nasty August day. The air was full of wasps and flies and bluebottles and they all seemed hungry for the bright pink flesh of Baron Fitzwater. The Baron sweated and swatted as a squad of ten mechanically-marching soldiers entered the hall without knocking and came to a halt within a few feet of his burning face. Their captain produced a scroll and read:

> *"To the Baron Fitzwater of Arlington. You have refused*
> *to pay the taxes which have been demanded of you in the*
> *King's name. I therefore take command of your estate,*
> *Arlington Castle, and all its furniture,*
> *by Royal Command of Prince John."*

The Baron stood and made a speech lasting three-quarters of an hour which you must imagine. It made no difference at all. A very brief argument followed, at the end of which the Baron found himself locked outside his own castle with a black eye and bruised backside.

He thought for a long time, then he swallowed down the last of his pride and walked towards Sherwood Forest.

Along the dusty road he met a group of tattered creatures resting under a tree. One had lost a leg, and one an arm, and one was blinded and another one was mad. They were young men who had gone on the Crusades with King Richard. Now they were trying to find their way home.

The Baron fumbled in all his pockets and gave the wounded men all the money he had. Then he hurried on his way to visit Robin and Marian.

He was greeted by the yapping of Hayrick and Stubbs and the appearance of a portly figure.

"Friar Michael," bawled the Baron, "you're fatter than ever!"

"By the flat feet of Saint Marmaduke, I'm pleased to hear it," his old friend replied. "But here in the forest I am Friar Tuck. Welcome to the palace of Robin Hood and Maid Marian."

"A palace without a roof?" asked the Baron.

"Why, no," replied the Friar. "Our palace has the most beautiful roof in the world, for it is painted deep blue and golden by day, and by night it is lit by the silver lamp of the moon and the thousand miniature candles of the stars. The palace floor is intricately woven from the green, white, yellow and blue of grass and daisies and primroses and violets. Its mighty columns are the oak and beech trees. The court musicians are the lark, the thrush, the linnet and the nightingale – "

"And me," interrupted Alan A-Dale, a touch grumpily.

"Then who's the King?" asked the Baron suspiciously.

"Robin Hood is King of the forest. He is the free choice of the people who live here. He rules over all the deer and wild boar."

"But he's not a real king like William the Conqueror in the old days," said the Baron firmly.

"Of course he is, by the shining bald dome of Saint Indigo," said Friar Tuck. "William fought to win the throne of England. Robin fought for Sherwood Forest. William raised taxes from the people. So does Robin – he takes money from the rich people who pass through Sherwood. Why did the people pay taxes to William? Because they were forced to. Why do they pay money to Robin? Because they have no choice. There's only one difference – King William took from the poor and gave to the rich. King Robin takes from the rich and gives to the poor. Little John is his Prime Minister and I am his Archbishop, by the strong breath of Saint Meniculous."

"Very true," said Robin Hood, who had come to greet the Baron. "But there is one thing missing in our court – a Queen. My lord, may I take Lady Matilda to be my wife here in my court and crown her with flowers of the wildwood?"

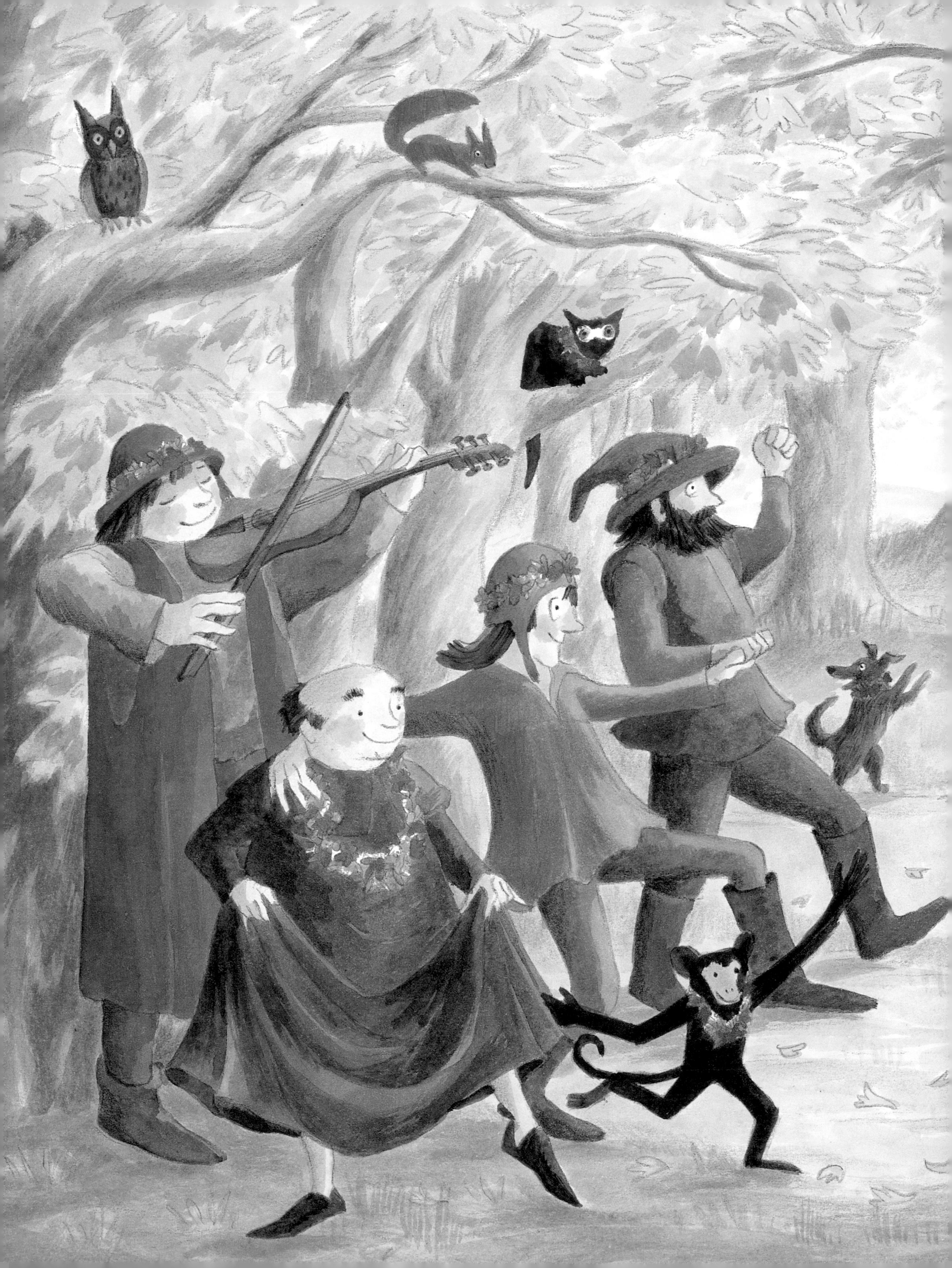

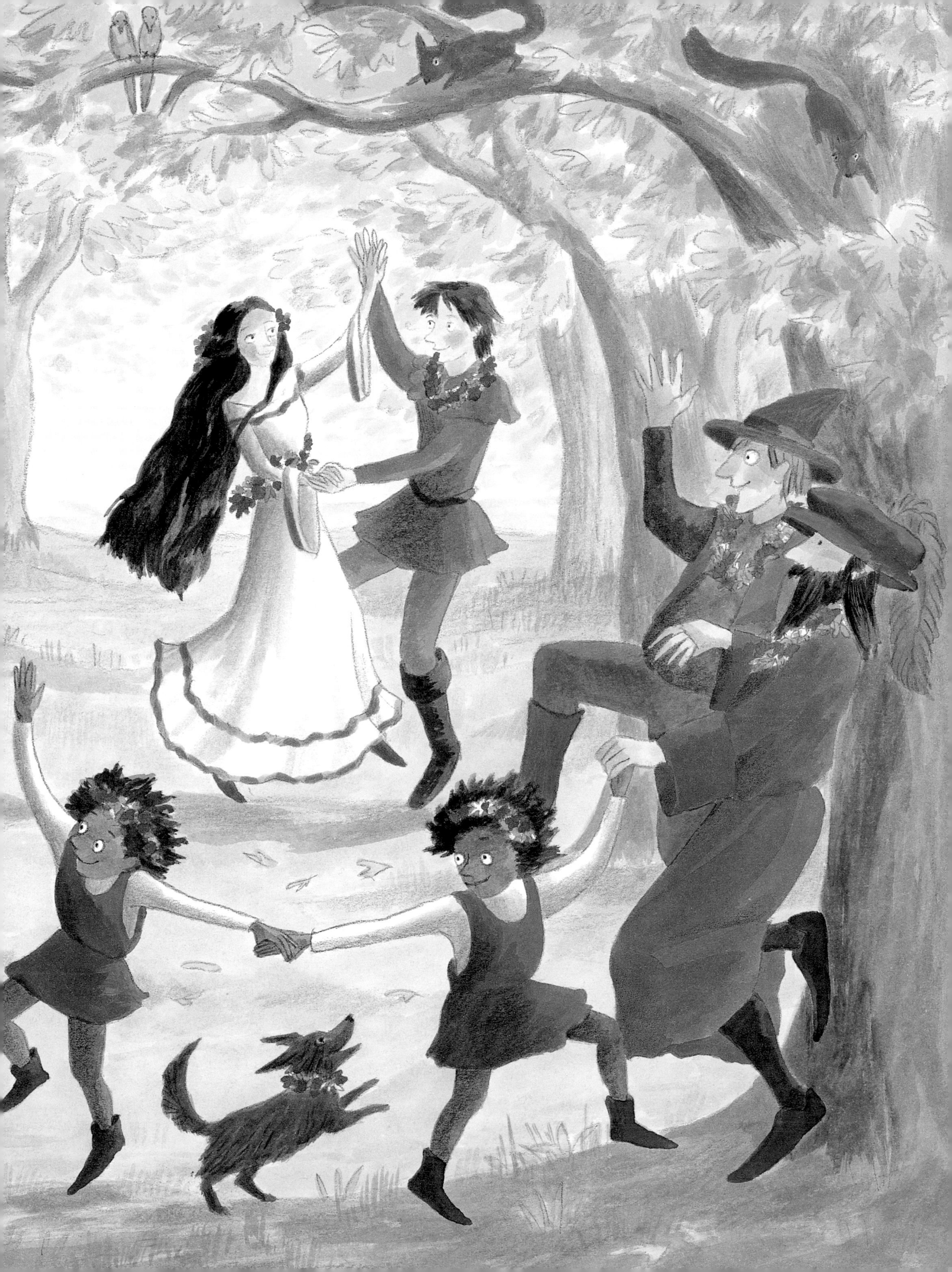

The Baron stared at the toes of his boots for a long time. Hayrick and Stubbs leaned affectionately against his ankles.

"Robin," said the Baron, "you are a good man and a brave man and the best king I ever heard of. If Matilda will have you, you may marry her." He nodded and shook hands with Robin.

So Robin and Marian were married by Friar Tuck in the green cathedral of Sherwood. Jenny Hoghig was their bridesmaid and Jemmy their pageboy. Then Little John played the fiddle while his monkey Harrietta danced, and then everyone danced and then they feasted and Much the Miller's son recited a poem he had written with doves and roses in it and Alan A-Dale sang a wedding song for Robin and Marian which was twenty-six verses long. And everyone, especially the Baron, joined in the chorus:

"We'll drink to Marian and Robin Hood
And their praises we will sing.
For theirs is the kingdom of the wild greenwood
And they are our Queen and our King."

The Last Arrow

It was a long, long time later and it was Christmas Day. In a rough forest shelter, warming their hands at a glowing log fire, sat Marian with her children, Alison and John. On her lap nestled Harrietta, now a silver-haired and dignified old monkey.

"Was our papa a very tough man?" was the next question, from John, who looked forward to the day when he would be strong enough to shoot a longbow.

"He was strong and he was gentle," said Marian. "He often lost fights, and when he did lose, he laughed and forgot it. He wasn't very interested in fighting. He was more interested in being free."

"But was he a good man?" asked Alison.

"Oh yes. He was an outlaw, but he was a saint. He only stole from rich people. He shared the money he stole with his friends and with the weak and helpless – the poor and the old and the sick all blessed his name and thought he was a kind of Saint Francis with a bow and arrow."

"Why did the outlaws take Robin as their leader if he lost fights?" asked John.

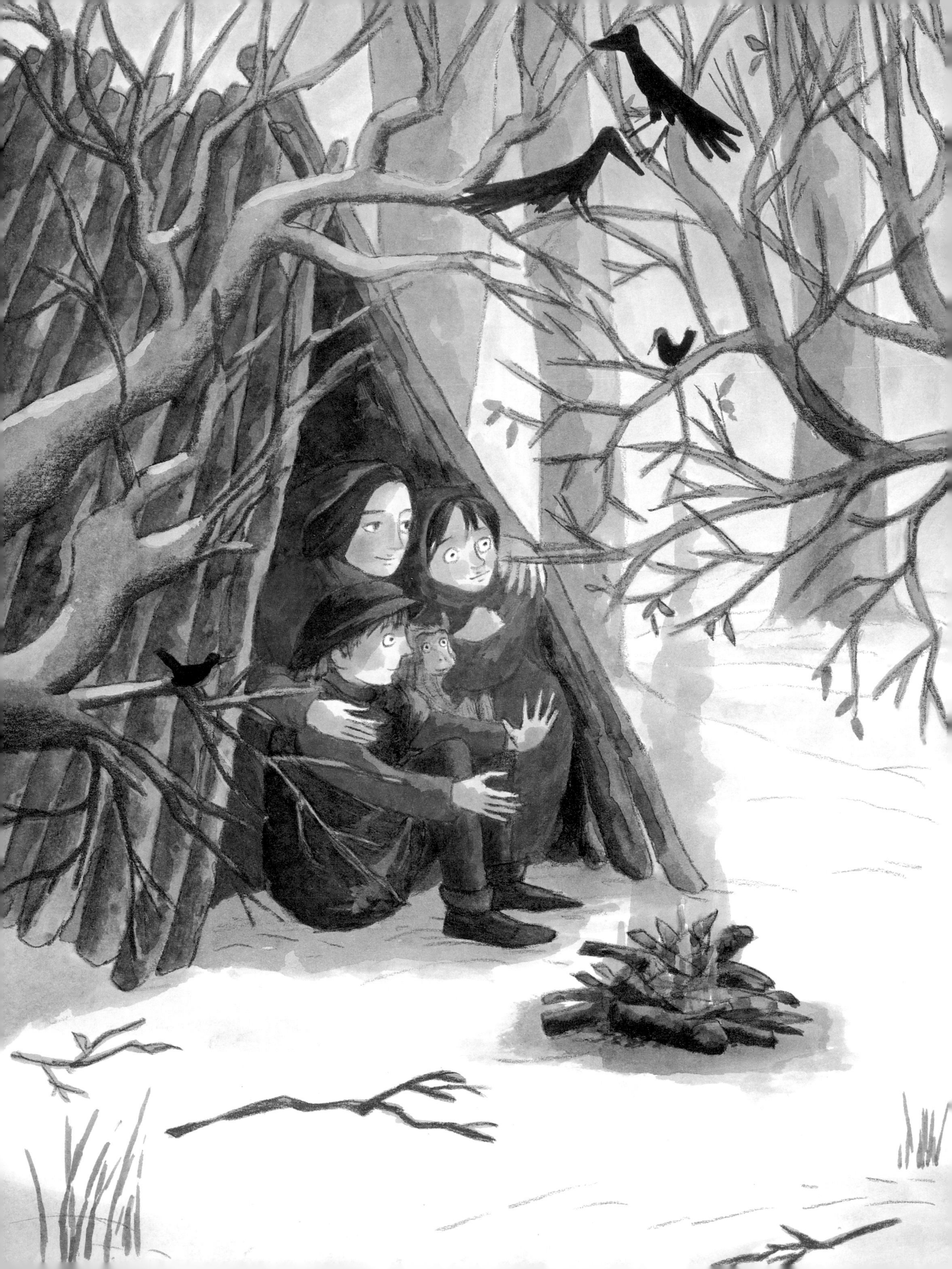

"I think it was that smile of his," said Marian, "that slow smile of his, like a sweet arrow through your heart. That smile meant he didn't have to give orders, because everybody wanted to please him by doing whatever he wanted to do. And, of course, he was the bravest man in the world."

"Tell us again how Papa died," said John. So Marian put her arms around her children and told them that old familiar story – although this time she ended with a secret they had never heard before.

"One day, in springtime, Robin was stricken with a hot fever. For three days he fought his illness, but in the end he had to give in and asked Little John to take him to somebody who would treat his sickness.

The great nunnery of Kirklees was well known as a hospital for fever patients. It was there that Little John took Robin and gave him into the charge of the Prioress of Kirklees.

Now Robin and Little John did not know that the Prioress was the sister of Sir Ralph Montfalcon who died in the swamp, and she nursed a great bitterness in her heart against Robin Hood.

The Prioress received them kindly. She led Robin up the winding stone stair to a room in a high tower, but she would not let Little John come with him.

Little John lay down in a little glade near by, from where he could watch the door of the nunnery, and stayed there like some great, faithful dog.

The Prioress helped Robin to a bed. She said he must be bled, which is the treatment for a bad fever. And she did bleed him, but the vein she opened with her sharp little knife was not a small blue one near the surface, but one of the deep veins through which the bright red blood runs leaping from the heart.

Then she turned and left him alone to bleed to death. She locked the door of the room behind her. All that day the blood ran from Robin's arm, and he couldn't stop it. He called for help, but no help came, for his voice was weak and Little John could not hear him.

Finally Robin managed to crawl from the bed and reach his bugle-horn. He sounded it three times with all his failing strength. I heard it from far away and began to run through the forest towards the nunnery.

But of course Little John heard it too. The Prioress fled from the nunnery. Little John ran up the winding stone steps to Robin's room and broke the locks of its door with one charge of his great shoulder.

There lay Robin on the bed, his face all white with the long bleeding. Little John bandaged the wound with strips torn from the bedsheets. So the bleeding stopped, but it was too late.

Then I came in. Robin knew me and embraced me. He asked me and Little John to raise him up so he might look out of the window at the forest he loved. So we lifted him until he sat up.

Robin gazed for a long time. Then he said: 'Little John, string me my good longbow and put it in my hands with a straight smooth arrow.' And Little John did as he was asked.

Then Robin said: 'Marian, I love you more than all the world. Little John, I love you more than all other men. I will fire this arrow out of the window. I beg you, find that arrow, and where it strikes, there let my grave be dug.'

Robin raised himself suddenly and sat upright. Some of his old strength came back. He drew the bowstring back as far as his ear – then let go the arrow through the open window.

But as it flew, he fell backwards into my arms and the life flew out of his heart. That is how your father died."

Alison and John had heard the story many times before and they loved it, although it always made them weep. But this time their mother told them something new.

"After we had carried Robin's body down the winding stone stair," said Marian, "I ran to find his arrow so we would know where to bury him. It had fallen only a few feet from the window in the graveyard of the nunnery.

I picked up the arrow, lying amid all those marble gravestones and statues of angels, surrounded by high grey stone walls, and I could not bear the thought of his body buried there.

So I carried the arrow with me a mile or so, to the great oak where Robin and I used to play when he was a boy and I was a girl, and I stuck the arrow deep in its bark so that everyone would believe that he had shot a most wonderful shot from his deathbed. And so that he could be buried underneath the tree he loved."

Marian, Alison and John all looked out from their shelter. On the far side of the clearing they saw the great oak and the simple green grave of Robin Hood. And, in the distance, they could hear the cheerful singing of Friar Tuck, Little John, Jenny and Jemmy as they carried towards the shelter the best Christmas dinner of them all – a gigantic pasty.